# Southern Dead

A MAX PORTER PARANORMAL MYSTERY

Stuart Jaffe

*Southern Dead* is a work of fiction. Names, characters, places, and incidents either are the product of the author's imagination or are used fictitiously, and any resemblance to any persons, living or dead, business establishments, events, or locales is entirely coincidental.

SOUTHERN DEAD


Cover art by Renata Lechner

ISBN 13: 978-1-963517-08-8

First Edition: January, 2022
First Hardcover Edition: February, 2024

For Glory

*This one wouldn't exist without you*

# Also by Stuart Jaffe

*Max Porter Paranormal Mysteries*

Southern Bound
Southern Charm
Southern Belle
Southern Gothic
Southern Haunts
Southern Curses
Southern Rites
Southern Craft
Southern Spirit
Southern Flames
Southern Fury
Southern Souls
Southern Blood
Southern Graves
Southern Dead
Southern Hexes
Southern Hart

*Nathan K Thrillers*

Immortal Killers
Killing Machine
The Cardinal
Yukon Massacre
The First Battle
Immortal Darkness
A Spy for Eternity
Prisoner
Desert Takedown
Lone Star Standoff
The Puppeteer
Blowback
Prime

*The Ridnight Mysteries*

The Water Blade
The Waters of Taladoro
Waterfire

*The Parallel Society*
The Infinity Caverns
Book on the Isle
Rift Angel
Lost Time
Pages of Glass
The Bold Warrior
City of Infinity

*The Malja Chronicles*
The Way of the Black Beast
The Way of the Sword and Gun
The Way of the Brother Gods
The Way of the Blade
The Way of the Power
The Way of the Soul

*Gillian Boone novels*
A Glimpse of Her Soul
Pathway to Spirit

*Stand Alone Novels*
After The Crash
Real Magic
Founders

*Short Story Collection*
10 Bits of My Brain
10 More Bits of My Brain
The Bluesman
The Marshall Drummond Case Files: Cabinet 1
The Marshall Drummond Case Files: Cabinet 2
The Marshall Drummond Case Files: Cabinet 3

*Non-Fiction*
How to Write Magical Words: A Writer's Companion
For more information, please visit ***www.stuartjaffe.com***

# Southern Dead

# Chapter 1

## THURSDAY

WITH ARMS FOLDED AND STOMACH RUMBLING, Max Porter leaned against his car and tried to listen. But the day had been long and slow. Most days were like that lately. Too few cases and those that did come their way had more to do with researching family heritage than dealing with the paranormal. Still, Max would rather be inside the house eating than listening to Ms. Brenda Byrd.

Sandra had just set dinner onto the table when all of this began. J, their youngest boy, had noticed the lady pacing in front of the driveway. A plump, middle-aged woman with a wide, dark face and a bright, yellow dress, she rubbed her hands and mumbled to herself — probably rehearsing what to say. PB, their eldest, showed no interest — he chose to ignore anything strange about his guardians or their work. Regular meals and a roof overhead outweighed whatever scam he suspected Max and Sandra were running.

But the woman outside kept up her nervous pacing, and even PB thought it a ridiculous intrusion on their dinner. Though Max encouraged everyone to ignore her, the Sandwich Boys repeatedly left the kitchen table to report on the woman. This might have gone on throughout the meal, but Sandra set her fork down and insisted that they go out to deal with the woman. Now, as Max's chicken parmesan grew cold, he had to wait for Ms. Brenda Byrd to get to the point.

"Are you sure you don't want to come inside?" Sandra said, gesturing to the house.

Brenda shook her head and lit up a cigarette.

The hot day had begun to wane, but the mosquitoes didn't get the message. Max slapped at his arm. Marshall Drummond, the Porters' partner, snickered as he floated by. The old ghost couldn't enjoy a hot meal or a strong drink, but he also avoided the problems of insects and other nuisances. Max figured he should let his friend have a moment of joy. Not that many to be had for a dead detective.

After a long drag, Brenda put away her cigarette pack and gazed up the road. The small homes lining the street did not show Winston-Salem at its best, more the struggling to survive side, but it hardly screamed poverty or crime. Still, Brenda shivered. "Is it okay if I'm out here? I don't want anybody calling the police on me."

"Why would anybody do that?" Max asked.

Brenda flashed a look of incredulity. "Because I'm a black woman hanging out in front of your house and I'm sure I look plenty agitated."

"Black people live on this street, too. But if you'd rather come inside like my wife suggested —" At least, then, Max could eat while they talked.

"No." She looked at the house like she expected the walls to bleed.

The sun dug into the horizon leaving the sky a mixture of light and dark, and an amber hue cast across the house. Max chilled. "Is there something wrong with our place? Is that why you're here?"

"Oh, not at all. I mean I don't know about your house, but that's not why I'm here." Her body slouched. "I'm sorry. I must look the perfect fool. To be honest, I'm a bit scared."

"Of our house?"

"Of going into the offices of the Porter Agency. I do that and I have to admit that something might be happening."

Sandra touched Brenda's arm. "But something is happening, right?"

"I think so. I think I'm haunted."

Drummond pushed back his fedora. "What a nice change. At

least we don't have to worry about the lady doubting in the supernatural."

"We're here to listen," Sandra said. "Go ahead and tell us why you came. I promise you'll feel better once you get it out."

Brenda nodded and took another drag on her cigarette. "I was raised a believer, and I've always been. Mama said there was magic in our bloodline, so I had to know all about the real world most people deny."

"She's a witch?" Drummond's pale visage shimmered, but Max tried not to look. Partly, he didn't want to be rude. Mostly, he didn't want to freak out Brenda by interacting with an empty space.

"What kind of bloodline?" Max asked.

"Mostly believers. But I think there was a voodoo priestess from New Orleans back during slavery. I don't know for sure about that, but everybody in my living family, as much as I can remember, has always known about magic and how some folk could use it to shape things." She flicked her cigarette butt into the street. "I'm telling you all this so you understand that I'm not some crackpot. I know about these things, same as you, and that's why I came here."

Sandra frowned. "You want us to cast a spell for you? We don't really do that."

Holding back a sarcastic laugh, Max readjusted against the car. The Porters had cast many spells over the years, and as Sandra continued exploring witchcraft, Max knew she cast many more. However, she spoke true enough — they did not cast spells for hire. That was the realm of witches and covens. Even if Sandra succeeded in becoming a good witch, she would still not be a mercenary of magic.

With a sudden inhale, Brenda found an ember of courage, and though the words trembled on her lips, she managed to speak. "I know better than to mess with such things. Spells and curses are too dangerous. No, I'm here because . . . I fear someone or something is trying to possess me. It has possessed me already."

"Well, now, that's interesting." Drummond settled next to Max, his ghost body halfway in the car door.

"It started with these dreams. Strange, dark things of a man being stretched and twisted. His pain vibrated the air around me, and sometimes I could barely breathe. He tried to speak, but all I could hear were these echoing cries. I'd be standing in a ballroom or sometimes a cavern, a big, empty, cold space, and he would emerge out of the dark corners and stretch towards me. It was a scary dream, but when I woke — the first time — I thought nothing more of it. Just a nightmare, really."

Max said, "Except it didn't stop."

"Not in the least. I suppose I could've learned to live with it, but after two weeks of that bad dream hitting me every night, I was like a zombie throughout the days. I couldn't get enough sleep and it was making me see and hear that stretched-out man all around me. Not like a full-on hallucination, but like a shadow just out of sight. There, but not there. I work for a property management firm, and it got so I didn't want to work late because I'd see the man in the dark. Driving home was risking my life. I could see him popping out from behind buildings and dropping down from the night sky."

"What's this man look like?" Sandra said. "Do you know him?"

"Not anybody I ever met. He's black. Graying a bit. And I think he's strong. Like he worked hard in his life. Oh, and he has a thick, white scar on his chin. When he stretches bad, that scar looks like a second mouth. It's horrible. But that's not the worst."

"What else happened?"

"I started sleepwalking. Same path every night. I have the nightmare and when I wake, I find myself standing outside my apartment building. I'm staring off down the road. But its seems like I walk a little further each night. That's why I finally broke down and came here. I'm afraid. If I don't stop this, some night, I'm going to walk out into the street and get hit by a car. Or worse — what if some night, he stretches right into my soul?"

Max had to admit he had stopped thinking about his empty stomach. Mostly. "Do you feel this man's presence now?"

"On it," Drummond said, whisking away to search the area.

With more subtlety, Sandra also gazed around. To Max, she made a tiny shake of the head.

"I never feel him," Brenda said. "Not until it's too late. Not until he's a passing shadow or in my dreams."

Drummond returned. "Nothing but the usual."

Holding back his desire to ask what *the usual* entailed, Max kept his attention on Brenda. "This is not a lot to go on. We're a research agency and so far, you haven't given us anything we can research."

"You're much more than that." Brenda opened her purse, reached for the cigarettes, but then thrust them back. "I know how this sounds. It's a bunch of scary dreams at night and things I can't quite see during the day. But I'm telling you I know what I know. Something is trying to get at me."

"We don't doubt you. We've seen enough bizarre things in our time that almost anything is worth checking out, but like I said, I don't see what we can actually research for you." He looked to Sandra. "Unless you know of a spell to observe her dreams."

"No such thing," Sandra said. "At least, not that I've ever come across. There are spells — curses, really — meant to put a thought in your head. Works sort of like an earworm, but that's a lot different than going into another person's dreams."

Brenda folded her hands over her stomach. With a patient tone that Max suspected came from years of being ignored, she said, "Please, listen. I'm not interested in you casting a spell. Magic is dangerous stuff, and I've been brought up well enough to know not to mess with it."

"Then what do you want us to do?" Max asked.

"Follow me." She looked down at her hands. "In case he gets more visible. More present. I don't know. In case he attacks me."

Sandra said, "There's nothing around you. I'm not denying that you're experiencing these things, but I don't think having us follow you is going to help any. It'll be a waste of your money."

Brenda wiped at her eyes. "You've got to help. There's got to be something you can do."

"I'm afraid my wife is right." The idea of getting a new client, of making money sounded great, but Max also knew Sandra had spoken the truth. "If you can get this man's name — the one in your dreams — or perhaps look around your house and see if there are any witch symbols. Anything that we could actually investigate for you, then we'll be happy to do so. But from what you've told us —"

"You're supposed to be the best. Everybody in the paranormal community knows it. If you have a real problem, the kind nobody will take seriously, then you go to the Porter Agency."

"The paranormal community?"

"It's the 21st century, Mr. Porter. Those of us who experience the supernatural don't sit at home fretting away. We get online and talk to each other. We connect. And we start groups that meet regularly to discuss this kind of thing. Surely, you've come across some of the ghost hunters out there. They were the start, but we have other groups now that actively work together to explore the paranormal world. At least, we discuss it."

Drummond clicked his tongue. "Well, how do you like that?"

"We're flattered," Sandra said.

Brenda glanced away. "I don't want to sound like I'm making a big deal of it. It's not like we're the North Carolina Paranormal Society. Those are the best. We're just a little group with a silly name that likes to chat about what might be out there."

"Silly name?" Max said.

"We call ourselves the Creeper Peepers." Brenda giggled off her embarrassment. "We are serious about it all, though."

"I'm sure you are," Sandra said, "but as my husband has pointed out, there just isn't enough to go on. We're not going to take your money for doing nothing."

"You will be doing something." Brenda looked up, her eyes glistening, her hands shaking. "I need peace of mind. I need to know that somebody is watching my back until this is dealt with. Besides, if you witness me sleepwalking, if you see one of these shadows during the day, you'll know I'm telling the truth."

"We don't doubt your honesty. We only doubt what we can do for you."

"Well, it's my money, and I'm willing to spend it on you."

Drummond snapped his fingers. "Can't really argue with that."

Max said. "If you're sure you want to spend your money this way, then I suppose we'll agree to help."

Rolling her shoulders back, Brenda's face brightened. "You will?" She lunged forward to shake Sandra's hand and then Max's. "Oh, thank you, thank you. I know it seems silly, but I promise this will be worth it. You won't regret it."

Sandra forced a smile. "If we do our jobs right, then there won't be anything to come of this. And I promise, we'll refund the money, if there's no real case here."

"Having you even consider my situation is worth every dime. It's peace of mind, I tell you, peace of mind." Brenda started another round of handshaking.

"If that's what we offer you," Max said, "then we'll do our best. Go home, and try to get some sleep tonight. We'll start in the morning."

Brenda hesitated, and Max worried she would insist on their participation that night. But instead, she nodded with an embarrassed grin. "Of course. Y'all were probably about to have supper. I'll be on my way. See you in the morning."

They stood in the driveway and watched Brenda cross the street, get in her car, and drive off. The moment their new client could no longer see them, Sandra turned toward Max and put her hand on her hip. "Are you serious?"

"What? She needs peace of mind, and we've got bills to pay."

She turned to Drummond. "You're okay with this?"

Lowering his Fedora, Drummond said, "I don't get involved in marital spats."

"This is not marital. It's business."

"In that case, I say there's no harm in watching her for a few days."

"There's big harm. First of all, she belongs to Creeper Peepers. I don't know anything about them, but I'm guessing they're not filled with actual witches or psychics or people like us who see ghosts."

"That's awfully presumptuous," Max said. "Just because you and Drummond didn't see anything around her, doesn't mean there isn't. Something's got her spooked."

"You would be, too, if you were suffering from insomnia to the point that you're hallucinating."

"Why are you so against this? What if she really needs our help?"

"Then we're here for her. I'm not against it — not exactly."

"I see. You're against her because she's not from the official North Carolina Paranormal Society. Her little club doesn't reach your standards."

"Hey, don't make me sound like a snob."

Drummond said, "Doll, you did sound a bit snobby there for a moment."

"I thought you stayed out of marital spats."

"I didn't realize we'd left the business conversation."

"Try to keep up." She paused to calm her voice. "If we take every crackpot case that comes our way, soon our reputation will go in the toilet."

"Until a few moments ago, we didn't even know we had a reputation."

"We know we have one amongst the real witches."

"That's sounding a bit snobbish again."

Before Drummond could turn a spat into a full argument, Max said, "We know she's already a believer. Smart one, too."

Sandra said, "Look, I simply feel that we should have more to go on than what she's given us before we start billing people."

"I know." Max pushed off the car and headed toward the house. "I agree with everything you've said. This case looks very thin and we have next to nothing to go on. I also agree we need to watch out for our reputation. We've worked hard for years and don't want to throw it away. But I also know that the real reason you're angry is because you're worried there might be something to this. That perhaps there is a type of ghost out there that you can't see. And if that's the case, then what else might be out there?"

Sandra paused. Her anger withered as her true concerns

bubbled up to the surface. "You really think there might be something like that?"

"I have no idea. But I know one thing — I'm starving. Let's go in and have dinner."

Despite herself, Sandra put her arm around Max. "After dinner, since you're the one so big on taking this case, you're going to give this woman her money's worth. Research her life and her family. If she's not being haunted, she should at least get a nice family tree or find out she's related to somebody famous."

From behind, Drummond said, "Don't worry about me. You all enjoy that food I can't taste. I'll just float out here until morning."

# Chapter 2

MAX AND SANDRA ATE IN SILENCE. Not an uncomfortable silence, but one with a question hanging between them. They were in strange territory — neither had been wrong, but neither had been right. At least, that was how Max saw it.

They needed the money. Plain and simple. Their home had been designed to start a newlywed couple and, maybe, their cat. Not a family of four. Plus, they really would bring some peace of mind to that poor woman. However, Max knew Sandra had been right, too. Creeper Peepers was not the North Carolina Paranormal Society by any quality measurement. If Brenda had worked with the latter, Sandra would have taken her seriously from the start. But this?

After finishing dinner and cleaning up, Sandra went off to read a book while Max settled into the back corner of the kitchen — his office. Firing up his laptop, he remembered when they were flush with money. Big house, two new cars, his own study, and an office in the city. But they also once lived in a trailer park. He wondered if they would ever get off this financial rollercoaster. At least, the next swing should bring them upward. He didn't think they had much further they could fall.

Then again, he knew there was always further to fall.

"You really got a sucker this time," PB said as he rifled through the refrigerator for a snack.

"Didn't you have dinner less than an hour ago?"

"Y'all are the ones telling me I'm a growing boy."

More a man than a boy, but Max didn't feel witty at the moment. Particularly because of the way PB saw their work. Over the years, it had never bothered Max too much. PB had yet to accept the existence of the supernatural, so it made sense that he assumed Max and Sandra ran a con job on susceptible people. However, the truth had to become clear to PB someday.

Only now, the boy might be right.

One way to find out for sure. Get to work.

Max found the basics quite fast. Born and raised in Winston-Salem, Brenda Byrd never left the city except for her college years at UNC Greensboro. She lived a decent, middle-class life, and while Max knew that she had to have suffered plenty of prejudice along the way, from all he found, she appeared to have been a well-adjusted and happy child.

In fact, Max discovered that in seventh grade, Brenda won second place for a schoolwide short story contest — a ghost story, of course — and her mother won a blueberry pie bake-off three years in a row. The only blemish in their lives was reported in the Winston-Salem Journal on October 10, 2002 — Mr. Luther Byrd died when a drunk driver swerved into his lane and hit him head on during the middle of the night.

After college, Brenda jumped from job to job and lived in a series of cheap apartments on the edge of the city. Eventually, she landed an entry-level position with a property management company. They focused mainly on college rentals, centering around Wake Forest University, but also servicing the smaller colleges as well as reaching out to Greensboro. Because of Brenda's involvement, the company had begun looking at property closer to Charlotte — a more lucrative but also more competitive area. They promoted her and she stayed with them ever since. Worked her way right up the ladder, and if they didn't offer her a partnership soon, she would have every right to believe that racism had bitten her once again.

Max tried to read between the lines, but he simply found nothing supernaturally suspicious. Brenda Byrd lived an average life, and if she behaved in any manner that would call upon the darker forces of nature, she had kept all record of it well hidden. Not an easy thing to do — especially on the internet. Even the most seasoned witches managed to leave behind a breadcrumb or two.

Looking at his notes, he said, "If it's not you directly, then I suppose I have to dig into your family."

First up — the father. Luther Byrd had died an unnatural death, so Max pulled up all the photos of the accident and of Mr. Byrd's car beforehand. Comparing before and after, zooming in on every blurry picture, Max hunted for any witch symbols, mojo bags, or other signs of witchcraft.

Nothing.

He moved on to the mother. According to newspaper obituaries (which he matched against county records), Myrtle Byrd died in early-2020. Cause of death — presumed COVID. Things were still early in the pandemic back then. Nobody knew exactly what they were dealing with, and there was no vaccine.

After her mother's passing, Brenda left her apartment and moved back into her childhood home. What Max could find on Myrtle did not point to witchcraft at all — other than a healthy knowledge of its existence.

Assuming Brenda was not imagining any of this, then perhaps her mother had been trying to reach out to her. But why couldn't Sandra or Drummond see the old woman? And why would Brenda's dreams be of a man? Be so terrifying? Surely the mother would want to send her daughter warm, peaceful images. Sensations of hope.

Next, the last person Max wanted to dive into — the voodoo priest from New Orleans.

Unfortunately, Max had so few specifics to go on and New Orleans had so many voodoo priests that he came up empty. Perhaps Sandra could find out more through her witch connections, but he didn't think much would come of it anyway. None of this spoke voodoo. For one thing, outside of the movies, voodoo was more a religion than a form of witchcraft. More importantly, voodoo was not subtle. If somebody had used a spell or ceremony to haunt Brenda with her old relative or something similar, there would be symbols and bones and chicken blood all over her home. Voodoo worked partially through the psychological. The priest or priestess wanted it to be known a spell had been cast.

"Maybe Sandra's right." Hearing the words out loud gave

them more solidity. He thought about another deep search into New Orleans, but his eyes stung from staring at the computer screen too long. More than that, he knew the feeling inside — that he was stretching, desperately reaching for some confirmation of an idea. That usually happened when he knew he was wrong. And that meant, they would have to give the money back.

Stacked on the left corner of his small desk, the pile of bills awaited him. He didn't have the mental energy that night to go through and compare against their bank balance, to figure out which could be paid and which could be pushed until they received another overdue notice, to suffer the too familiar anxiety of wondering if they would be able to survive one more month in this dump of a house.

His phone rang. His mother.

Wonderful.

"Max, dear, I hate to bother, but would you please pick up a few items for me? I'm a little low on a couple things, and I won't even be able to have breakfast in the morning without them."

Trying to hide the whine in his voice — or the perturbed growl — Max said, "I'll get whatever you need first thing in the morning. I can have it all to you before you wake up."

She laughed without any humor. "Honey, I wake up ahead of the sun. And I like to have my oatmeal and fruit and a glass of orange juice first thing. I need all of that. The stores are still open for a few hours, but nobody's going to be open at four in the morning."

"I promise I can get you what you need —"

"Never you mind. It's clearly too much of a burden. Besides, I have to take care of myself, right? I can do it. It'll be fun. I haven't had a chance to drive in a while. Of course, driving at night is a different matter, but you know I'm dying anyway, so what's the harm with a little risk?"

"You're not dying —"

"I have MS. I will die from it eventually."

"Yes, but not tonight."

"When you told me you'd be the one to help me through all

of this MS business, I thought you meant it. I should've known. Nobody wants to hang around an old lady like me, especially when you can smell the death on her."

"Stop talking like that. You've got many more years ahead of you."

"Not pleasant ones. Especially when all I want is a few minor things to make my morning brighter and I can't even get that."

Max clamped his mouth tight and closed his eyes. After counting to ten, he said, "Give me the list. I'm on my way."

# Chapter 3

UNPACKING THE GROCERIES picked up from a gas station convenience store, Max rolled his stiff neck. His body craved to lay down for the night. Wearing a periwinkle nightgown, Mrs. Porter stood in the kitchen doorway so as not to crowd her son, and he appreciated the small gesture. That much kindness did not extend to her flow of comments, though.

"I don't see why this has to be so hard for you," she said, ignoring his sighs and huffs. "Let me give you a regular list and you can pick any day of the week to do my shopping."

"That's what I suggested over a month ago." He thrust a box of saltine crackers into the cabinet. "But you said you couldn't possibly know what you would need week-to-week."

"Can you blame me? I'm still learning how to cook for one. Until now, I always had to be ready to feed you or the boys or visitors. Ever since my diagnosis, it doesn't seem like I have so many to cook for anymore."

"That's not true, and you know it. PB is here several times a week, and I'm stopping by practically every day."

"For a few minutes. Just to make sure that I'm still alive."

Max started to respond but checked himself. Anything he said would get twisted.

"You see? Your silence proves that you know I'm right."

With the last of the items stashed away, Max faced his mother. He opened his mouth but stopped once more. She had aged ten years in the months since learning she had MS. She looked smaller, a little hunched, deeper wrinkles, and grayer hair.

He walked up and hugged her. "I'm sorry. I don't mean to make you feel alone. You know I love you. I'll try to spend more time here."

"Don't feel obligated. I'm a grown woman. I can handle myself."

"I know." Still holding her, he cringed at the words leaving his mouth. "Have you given any thought to what I said last week? About you moving in with us? It would solve a lot of your complaints."

She stiffened. In a quiet voice, she said, "I don't think now is the right time."

Max kissed her forehead and tried to choke back the argument welling in his throat. He walked to the door. "That's fine for now. But there will come a day when you have no choice in the matter."

Her eyes blazed. "That may be, but I do have a choice today. I am not giving up my apartment. Besides, your house is too small."

"It is small, but the boys are teens now. Pretty soon they'll graduate high school and go on to whatever's next."

"College. That's what is next."

"Perhaps."

"What do you mean *perhaps?* They have to go to college."

"I'm not getting into that with you. They've both got a couple years before anything has to be decided. The point is that we can squeeze together now, and down the road, we'll have plenty of room."

She bristled. "Sounds wonderful. Truly riveting. Of course, Sandra hates me, so I'm fairly certain she'll make me feel most welcome."

"You've never given her a chance. Being under the same roof will give you an opportunity to see that she's a wonderful woman. She's kind and tough and caring and everything you would want for your son to have in a wife."

"I wanted grandchildren."

"You have PB and J."

"And I love them. But I never got to hold them as babies. I never go to help shape them as toddlers. They see me more of an old lady friend than a grandmother."

Max opened the front door and inched toward the hallway.

"I'd love to stay and argue with you, but I need to get to sleep. We picked up a new client today, and I've got work to do bright and early tomorrow."

"A client?" She paused. "I suppose you won't be around for a while."

"PB will be here tomorrow. You can look forward to that."

She brushed at her nightgown. "PB's a good boy. He actually cares about me."

Calling upon all his inner-strength, all his will power, he refrained from slamming the door shut. "I care," he said, the words rumbling low at first and building as he spoke. "But I also have to keep a roof over my family's head, food on the table, and make sure you're okay. I have to make hard choices, and I have to consider how that makes choices for others."

"No need to raise your voice. That will only get you full of adrenaline, and then you won't be able to sleep. Remember, you've got a big, new client tomorrow."

Plastering a smile so as not to scream, Max leaned close and kissed his mother on the cheek. "Goodnight," he said before rushing down the hall.

# Chapter 4

## FRIDAY

"I DON'T MEAN TO SOUND SO CRUEL," Max said to Drummond as they drove several car-lengths behind Brenda Byrd. He had slept little and now relied on caffeine to keep him going. Though awake, he could feel his fingers jittering against the wheel and his mouth moving faster than it should. "I know my mother has a lot to deal with considering the MS and all, but she deliberately tries to irritate me. Why? What's the upside for her?"

Tipping back his hat and hovering a hair above the passenger seat, Drummond clicked his tongue. "I would never claim to fully understand the better half of mankind and that goes double when discussing motherhood, but I will say this much — moaning about it to me won't change a thing. Might I suggest you take a page from my generation and swallow it down until you have time to deal with it proper."

"Your generation would swallow it down and deal with it never."

"Sounds like the proper time to me."

Brenda worked her way out of the city, cut through one of the ritzier sections of homes, and ended up on Stratford Road with shopping strip after shopping strip lining all the way to Hanes Mall. Apparently, she had the day off from work. Unless her company owned some of the commercial properties along Stratford, but from all Max had learned that did not seem likely. They focused on apartment rentals.

"All I'm trying to say —"

"Partner, I know exactly what you're saying. I'm dead, not

dumb. But you need to recognize that this is going to be a long, boring stakeout because we know our target, Ms. Byrd, is not going to commit a crime. That's usually the exciting point of a stakeout. You follow a guy, watch him, and wait for him to either do something bad or have something bad done to him. But this — she's running errands and we get to see all of the glorious, mundane action. So, please, stop making it worse by going on about your mother."

They turned down a steep and cracked lot, then parked in front of Jo-Ann Fabrics. As Brenda walked in, Max leaned back. He closed his eyes.

"What are you doing?" Drummond said. "We've got to pay attention."

"You don't want me talking, and I barely slept last night. I'm catching some shuteye. Wake me if something happens."

Folding his arms, Max shifted onto his side and tried to sleep. But he knew it wouldn't happen. Not when he could hear a ghost grumbling with every nonexistent breath.

Still, even without sleep, it felt good to have his eyes closed. The way life had been treating them lately, he would settle for whatever small pleasures came along. It wasn't Drummond's fault, though. Nor his mother's. Nor Sandra or PB or J or anybody. The simple fact was that the strain of being without money, of not knowing if they could keep paying rent on the house, of having no idea when the next paycheck might come — it all piled upon itself, creating a weight that always pressed upon his shoulders. Sandra's shoulders, too. But even sharing these burdens, they both felt the tension. Add to that a pandemic, and they were lucky to still have a business. Brenda Byrd was their first client in a long time.

As much as he hated to admit it, the Porters owed their current survival to Cecily Hull. She had forced Max into being on a retainer of sorts which provided some steady income. Not a lot. Not enough to assuage all worry, but better than nothing.

And she brought worries of her own. With her witch, Madame Ti, she worked to control the witches of North Carolina like her family had done for over a century. Or maybe she sought some other goal — one Max could not see yet.

"Wake up. She's out."

Max lifted his head and saw Brenda heading to her car. They followed her back onto Stratford, then a right onto Hanes Mall Boulevard, all the way past the restaurants and Home Depot, along the few curves of the road, until she made a left into the movie theater. She parked, bought a ticket, and entered the building.

Drummond said, "Now you might want to catch some shuteye. She'll be in there for a couple hours." He shook his head. "I told you this would be a boring job."

"Yeah, I'm sorry. I don't think we'll get much out of this situation."

"There is one strange thing."

"Oh?"

"For a lady who was on the verge of a mental breakdown last night, she sure seems calm and composed today. Running errands without so much as a glance behind her. Now, she's relaxing to a movie. Not the actions of a paranoid woman fearing she might get possessed."

"Not so strange if she's simply jerking us around."

A knock on the passenger side window startled both man and ghost. Max glanced through Drummond to see a police badge and ID pressed up against the glass — Detective Jorge Osorio. Before Max could look closely at the photo, the badge vanished and the car door opened.

A portly man with a thin mustache and long hair tied back leaned his head in. "Mind if I sit down?" He didn't wait for an answer.

"Not much for manners," Drummond said as he drifted to the backseat.

Osorio wore brown slacks and a white shirt, both of which were wrinkled, and he rested a shoulder satchel across his belly. He put out his hand. "Good afternoon."

Max shook the hand and bit back the flood of comments filling his head. Instead, he parroted the man. "Good afternoon."

"You can relax. You're not in trouble. Not yet, anyway."

Osorio grinned, and when he turned his head, a small stud in his earlobe sparkled. "But I'd be lying if I said I'm not concerned for you. That's why I'm sitting here. I want to do you a favor and help you out of a jam you're in."

"A jam? I don't think you've got the right car."

Osorio laughed like a mediocre actor on stage. "Oh, I know exactly where I am."

Drummond said, "I already don't like this guy. Let me chill his brain and you can dump him."

"Perhaps it would help," Max said, "if you told me what you want."

"That should be obvious. I've been following you all morning — watching you as you watch Ms. Byrd. I'm here to tell you that you're making a big mistake. You don't want to mess with her."

"No?" Max tried to sound confident yet confused. Not too hard considering it was mostly true. At least, the *confused* part.

"You related to one of her victims? Or do you consider yourself a vigilante?"

"Victims?"

Osorio drummed his fingers on the satchel. "Okay, if you want to play it close to the vest, I'll play along. How about this — I'll show you the photos and in return, you explain to me why you're spending the day following around a murderer."

# Chapter 5

THOUGH A SCOFFING LAUGH crept up Max's throat, he managed to keep it from escaping. The look in Jorge Osorio's eye brooked no humor. Even Drummond held back from a witty wisecrack.

With a sharp sniffle, Osorio pulled back the satchel flap and dug out a file folder. From that, he produced several photographs which he handed over one by one. The photos shook in his hands.

The first revealed a small apartment from the main entranceway. Two chairs had been turned over. A red couch cushion rested across the room against the wall. The coffee table in front of the couch had been smashed, and several pictures on the walls hung cockeyed. Though far from being an expert, Max had no trouble understanding that these were signs of a struggle. Somebody fought hard against an attacker. But Max noted a lack of blood.

He picked up the second photo — the front door. No splintered jamb. No broken chain lock. Nothing to suggest the door had been forced open.

The final picture presented Max with a High School photo of a young woman wearing a graduation gown and posed in front of a generic blue-white background. Brunette, thin bordering on anorexic but not sickly, light freckles across the nose, whisps of eyebrows over pale blue eyes. She smiled for the camera — a genuine smile that promised a bright personality. Probably not the most popular girl in school but well-liked and the kind to avoid the most dangerous pitfalls of youth.

"Ashley Cortez," Osorio said. "Eighteen. Just got her first apartment and was getting ready to start college at Winston-Salem State University. Last week, she called her father all worried that somebody was following her. Just an uneasy feeling, really, but her father had taught her to never ignore such feelings, her instincts. So, she called him to help."

Max stared at the smiling face so excited about her future. "What could her father do?"

"Didn't I mention it? He's my friend. Jake Cortez. We met years ago, back when there was a suspicious death at his office building. That time turned out to be nothing, but we stayed in touch. Both of us like to play golf, and well, there it is. He called me — worried for his daughter. I told him I'd look into it, and if I could find anything to give cause, I'd have a uniformed officer placed out front of her apartment on protection duty until we settled the matter." Osorio paused, breathing heavy as he looked down at Ashley's photo. "I promised I would talk with her in the morning. Never got the chance. She was abducted that night."

"Cute kid," Drummond said, leaning forward enough to chill the back of Max's neck. "What's the connection to our client?"

Max said, "You obviously think Brenda Byrd kidnapped your friend's daughter."

"At first. But it's rare, exceedingly rare, for a kidnap victim to still be alive a week after an abduction when there's never been a ransom call or any evidence to point us toward where she was being held captive. I won't tell Jake this — though he's no fool; I'm sure he's figured it out. The only bit of hope we've still got is that a body hasn't turned up."

"But why Brenda? What's her connection to this girl?"

"Ashley had some, well, darker interests."

Drummond snapped his fingers and pointed at Osorio. "There it is. Trouble always hits people messing around with magic and not knowing what they're doing."

"Such as?" Max asked.

Osorio said, "She believed in witches and magic, all kinds of supernatural things. I think her parents looked at it like a harmless, macabre phase. Like when she became a Goth kid. But then she joined this occult group. Same one as Brenda Byrd."

Max choked on a laugh. "The Creeper Peepers? They are hardly dangerous people."

Raising his chin, Osorio had a cocky gleam in his eye. "You'd think that, and I don't blame you. All the detectives I know that have come across the Peepers think the same way. Heck, I did as well. Until I looked into Ms. Byrd."

"Why her? There are others in the group."

"I've looked into a few of them. Anybody who had been identified as a friend of Ashley's. But of them all, Ms. Byrd is the one who keeps being connected to other occult crimes. Just last year, when the city was finishing up its reworking of Business 40 — the part that cuts through the city — there was an incident on the construction site. A man had fallen off one of the unfinished bridges and died. Thing was that we found an entire cult set up under the completed bridge just up the way. A weird pentagram painted on the ground, cloaks and the smell of something burnt. There were a few people there, too — out of their minds with their babbling about magic."

Max swallowed hard, hoping he didn't betray any surprise. "Really? I hadn't heard about that." He thought he sounded sincere as he searched Osorio's face for any hint that the detective might actually know the truth — that he had described one of the Porter's cases.

"Be careful," Drummond said. "This guy might be fishing."

The desire to whip around and glare at the ghost had to be suppressed. Especially when Osorio continued, "We got a lot of the details kept from the press, but there's no doubt that had been an occult situation. More recently, there was an incident at a Fourth Street parking lot across from the old YMCA. Used to be an old building that was demolished years back and nothing much ever happened there but parked cars. Then one morning we get a bunch of calls about an electrical storm in that spot. Only that spot. Strange hallucinations, too — flying cars, mini-hurricanes, that kind of thing. We originally thought there had to be some kind of gas leak or chemical spill, but when I went out there, I found the leftovers of another magic circle like the one under the bridge. Somebody had done a quick job of covering it up, but I found it. For the life of me, I can't figure out how they pulled off that stunt, but they freaked out a lot of the local residents."

Another Porter case. Max forced calm interest mixed with a bit of extra curiosity and a dash of doubt. "You think these were both done by this group Brenda and Ashley belonged to? The Creeper Peepers?"

"Like I said — you'd think they're harmless, but there was also blood found at the parking lot. Enough to suggest to my mind that somebody had been killed there and moved."

"But you never found a body."

"No. Both cases were closed. But that doesn't mean we got it right. And now, with Ashley missing, I'm starting to see a new pattern."

Drummond said, "Uh-oh. This detective isn't just working the missing person case. He's going outside of official channels on this. You better be extra careful."

"A new pattern?" Max asked as if he had no clue what Osorio meant.

"Brenda Byrd, of course," Osorio said, taking back the photographs and stuffing them in his satchel. "I've traced her movements, and while I can't put her at the crime scenes yet, I'm getting close. She's involved."

"And that makes her a murderer?"

"Call it my detective instincts. I've been watching her. That woman is filled with guilt. Really. Can't sleep through the night. Can't function throughout the day without looking over her shoulder. Even if she didn't commit the killings herself, she knows who did. She participated in some manner. And now, she's the only link I have to any criminal element connecting with Ashley."

Max raised his eyebrows as he said, "I don't know what you want from me, but I've got nothing to say. She hired me yesterday to follow her around, sort of like protection, I guess."

"You see, then? She is worried. Must be scared of others in her little cult."

"Maybe. But it doesn't sound like you have any hard evidence against her." He gestured to the movie theater. "She's not done anything suspicious all day — which you probably know from following us around."

Osorio handed over his business card. "I hope you're telling me the truth about your involvement here. Because I'm telling you that I know what I'm talking about. Something's not right with her, and I've got a strong gut feeling it connects to Ashley Cortez. You be careful. Brenda Byrd might be a dangerous killer. You find out anything, you call me."

"Of course." Max pocketed the card.

"And if you're lying to me, you better pray I never see you again."

Leaving that threat hanging in the air, Osorio slipped out of the car. Drummond drifted back to the passenger seat, moving about as if he needed to readjust after having Osorio change things — though the living detective touched nothing and the dead detective couldn't touch anything.

"Looks like you got a lot more researching to do," Drummond said.

"Yeah. About Brenda Byrd and Jorge Osorio."

"Seeing that this stakeout is not going anywhere interesting and you've got time to spend on your computer, I'm thinking the best use of me is to go follow our new detective pal. See if I can't dig up what he's really all about."

Max nodded. "Good thinking. Get on it and I'll meet with—" But Drummond had already vanished.

# Chapter 6

TAMPING DOWN THE URGE to storm into the movie theater and demand Brenda deliver the truth, Max returned to his laptop, hoping to dig up answers in her past or the Porter Agency's old cases. He had at least an hour before any movie ended. Deciding to start with the old cases — he needed a change after spending so much time sifting through Brenda's life — Max pulled up the file on the inhuman spirit and the Brotherhood of the Rising.

That case ended in the Fourth Street parking lot, but it began at the Reynold's family home which had been turned into a museum — Reynolda House. He clicked through one photo after another, searching for anything that might connect to Brenda Byrd or Ashley Cortez. The spells that Sandra had employed had nothing to do with the kind of experiences Brenda relayed, and nothing in the case involved kidnapping. Although, the Brotherhood did hire a paranormal investigative team under false pretenses. They were mostly novices but legit in their approach. Not a fringe group like the Creeper Peepers.

The other case Osorio had mentioned involved a cult led by PB's biological father. Max had far less to look through on that one. He had been too wrapped up in saving his son to take proper notes and documentary photos. However, part of that case involved the Lawson family massacre in which Charlie Lawson slaughtered six of his children on Christmas morning in the 1920s. There were plenty of photos online of that house and that family. Max also found plenty of photos showing the highway construction including the bridge where PB's father plummeted to his death.

None of it, however, connected to Brenda or Ashley. He kept thinking he would see one of their faces in the background of a newspaper photo, but no. Max found nothing to suggest that either young lady had any link to the Porter Agency cases.

And why should it? Osorio saw a connection because he needed one and had no other reasonable explanation. But that was only due to a lack of facts. If Osorio had known about witches and spells, he would be drawing different conclusions.

Which meant that Max had to review all he had found on Brenda Byrd and hope he could uncover something he had missed. Then again, perhaps he should be hoping not to find anything at all. In fact, the best outcome would be that Osorio and Brenda were both wrong. Max could close the case, send a bill for his time, and with any luck, get a real case worthy of the Porter Agency's efforts.

Yet as he crawled through Brenda's work history, a part of him could not dismiss Osorio entirely. Those photographs the detective had shown — of Ashley Cortez's disturbed apartment and of Ashley Cortez. The latter looked full of joy and promise, a young mind eager to race into her future. The former promised an unhappy conclusion to that jaunt.

If Brenda was as innocent as Max thought, then Ashley needed help. And if Brenda was the killer Jorge Osorio thought, then Max might be the one needing help.

As if responding to his darkening mood, the theater let out, and Brenda walked to the parking lot with a handful of other afternoon moviegoers. Max watched her closer than before, trying to detect the behaviors Osorio had indicated — the guilty looks over the shoulder, the uneasy movement brought on by the weight of diabolic actions. But she appeared to be an average woman. Perhaps a bit unsteady from insomnia, perhaps a bit wary of her surroundings, nothing more.

Driving a few cars back, Max did what he had been hired to do — he followed her. She headed toward the downtown section of the city but stuck to back roads and side streets. From the theater, she could have hopped onto the highway and zipped right into the heart of Winston-Salem. Instead, she weaved through one small neighborhood after another. When they passed schools, she dutifully slowed according to law. At four-way intersections, she came to a complete stop and waited a second or two before moving on. She drove as if she saw a police car directly behind her and wanted to avoid being pulled over.

They went through an upscale area filled with brick-faced McMansions that Max recognized right away. He and Sandra once owned one of these homes. Did Brenda know that? She certainly knew Max was following her. Had she driven by the spot where his old house had burned down on purpose? Perhaps as some sort of message — a threat.

Max shook off the thought. Osorio's suspicions were getting into his head, twisting everything around the remote possibility that Brenda was dangerous. Still, as he drove by the house — rebuilt as if nothing had happened and now home to somebody who owned a Tesla — Max couldn't silence the whispers wriggling at the back of his head like worms turning fertile soil. Something was off.

Back onto Silas Creek Parkway, over to Wake Forest University, then skirting the edges of the city until Brenda finally cut inward. She worked her way to the south-eastern side where the signs were in Spanish and the Mexican restaurants were fantastic. From there, she parked on a narrow road and walked up to a two-story building with ten apartments — five to a floor. Apparently, she lived in the middle on the second floor.

Max drove around the block three times until he lucked into a parking spot with a good view of the building. He pulled out his laptop and eased back the seat a bit. Though he peeked up from time to time, he had no expectation that Brenda would leave in the next few hours. Hopefully, he would make better use of the day by discovering something significant about Detective Jorge Osorio.

Much like Brenda, Osorio proved to be easy research. The man had posted much of his life on Facebook and Instagram. College photos with his buddies and his sweetheart at the time. Large family gatherings. Wedding photos. Wearing his police cadet uniform — fit and trim. Police Department baseball team — Osorio played third base many years back. First day as a detective. And progressive yearly photos that showed the man gently put on weight and lose some of his spark.

Osorio had other family in law enforcement, too. Of his two brothers, one had been a cop with the Highway Patrol. He died from a gunshot during a routine stop. Turned out the driver was a drug mule, car thief, and riding a cocaine high. Osorio's other brother had stayed clear of such dangerous work and built a life as a dentist. But their grandfather had been a cop to the bone. Never went in for detective — perhaps prejudice against Hispanics prevented that at the time — but made a good life from being a solid officer. There was also a cousin, Raquel, who had recently been promoted to Vice.

Max checked that Brenda's car had not moved and watched her apartment for a bit. Digesting the life of Jorge Osorio took some thinking. The man that Max had encountered did not exactly match the man that he had read about. Of course, nobody tells their full story on social media. Most people focus on the positive in their lives. Show off the good as if every day could be filled with nothing but happiness and adventure. Most don't post that they lied today or beat their kids or got drunk trying to forget the horror of the daily grind.

If he had the computer skills to hack into the police computer systems, Max wondered what he might find in Osorio's service files. Looking over the man's performance reviews would, no doubt, prove interesting. Instead, he would have to be content with what he could uncover through the public record. Thankfully, he had the skills to dig deep in that arena.

His initial searches through city newspapers brought up several noteworthy points. Many older papers from the 1970s and into the 1980s carried regular police logs of the previous night's incidents and arrests. From these, Max discovered that Osorio's grandfather had cleaned up his neighborhood nearly single-handed. It seemed whatever day Max looked at, there was Juan Osorio's name as the arresting officer of a petty thief, a drug dealer, a prostitution ring, or even the simple disorderly conducts.

When Osorio received his first commendation, a website focusing on the Hispanic community interviewed his mother. At one point, she said, "Osorio idolized his grandfather who had been a police officer, too. Sitting on the couch and listening to his grandfather tell story after story about fighting crime must have seeped into the boy's blood. It seemed like he always wanted to be a policeman."

As a detective, Osorio had done an outstanding job. He had an excellent closing rate on his cases and was even decorated for his part in a shootout during a bank robbery.

"Something had to have happened," Max said to the screen. After all, the Jorge Osorio he had met in his car did not resemble this paragon of policemen.

Max's phone rang — Sandra. After updating her, she remained quiet for a moment. Just when he opened his mouth to ask if she was okay, she said, "None of this makes much sense. If Brenda did the things this detective says, then why would she hire us?"

"Maybe she's crazy."

"Except I've been looking into types of hauntings to see if there could be a ghost that wasn't visible to me or Drummond."

"And?"

"It's not unheard of, but it's exceedingly rare. Normally, if a ghost or spirit wanted to possess a human being, it would have a visible form. But there are cases — mostly anecdotal — that suggest various reasons for an invisible ghost to be able to possess a person. None of them are good."

"So, Brenda might be making it all up."

"Or not."

"Or she's a killer."

"Or not."

Max rubbed his jaw. "I guess we'll both have to dig deeper."

"Don't forget about dinner tonight. You promised J we'd go out."

"I know."

"And honey, please, be careful."

"I'm hearing that a lot, lately."

Max checked that Brenda's car had not moved. He could see lights on in her apartment and the occasional shadow of her walking about. Returning to his work, he narrowed his searches to more recent activity about the detective.

A drop in the car's temperature announced the return of Drummond. "Partner, I don't know what to say. I followed Detective Osorio, and he seems clean. A good cop, too. Not on the take as far as I could see today. From the way he talked to other officers and his chief, I'd be shocked to find there was a bad bone in his body."

"Yeah, I'm finding much the same." Max continued clicking through newspaper articles. "It doesn't make sense, does it? I mean, tell me if I'm wrong, but the way this guy came into my car, the way he spoke with me, showing me case file photos, none of that was sound procedure. And his reasoning to peg Brenda Byrd with a kidnapping and potentially murder — it doesn't mesh with the portrait of the cop that I read about in the papers. An effective, by the book guy that builds strong cases for the DA to slam dunk."

Tapping his chin, Drummond said, "You're not wrong."

"When you were with him this evening, did you see him work on the kidnapping case?"

"Come to think of it, no. He had a body found in a dumpster which took most of his day."

"The chief allowed that? Wouldn't a missing girl take priority?"

"It should." Drummond clicked his tongue. "Unless nobody else knows about it."

"You think he's doing this off the books?"

"I'm starting to."

"Well, maybe we'll need to —" Max's skin prickled as he stared at the laptop screen.

"Partner?"

Reading from the article, Max said, "*Many of Winston-Salem's finest joined the cities elite families for a fundraiser to benefit the loved ones of fallen officers.*" With his fingers, he zoomed in on the photo. "Look at that."

Ten police officers stood in a line, each wearing their dress uniforms, each holding their caps at their sides, each straight-backed and smiling sternly. In front of them, five civilians in expensive clothes sat, stiff and proper. Three men and two women. The woman on the far right had a mysterious grin, barely perceptible, but to Max, it screamed out to be noticed — after all, he had seen it many times.

"Cecily Hull," Drummond said.

"That can't be good."

"Just because he was in the same room with her doesn't mean—"

"In our line of work? It kind of does."

Drummond sighed. "Yeah."

The computer's alarm rang out. Time to meet Sandra and J for dinner, but Max had lost his appetite.

# Chapter 7

AFTER A FEW INTENSE ROUNDS of Rock, Paper, Scissors, the choice of where to eat fell to J. He decided on Red Robin — a glorified burger joint attached to the Hanes Mall parking lot. Flatscreens had been mounted throughout, each broadcasting sports or music videos. Families made up the majority of diners, and the staff kept everything moving at a brisk pace.

For burgers, Max thought it inordinately expensive. Apparently, placing the word *gourmet* in front of a burger's name allowed one to charge ten dollars more than appropriate. Then again, seeing the pleasure on J's face and the satisfaction on Sandra's increased the value exponentially. Though paying for it would hurt their bone-dry finances, sometimes they simply needed to live a little better than money would allow — to keep sane, if nothing else.

Swallowing down a bite of mushroom-Swiss burger, J grinned. "I like when we have a case to work on."

"We're not sure if we're taking the case," Sandra said.

"We are. I can tell. Max is always happier when working a case. Less stressed."

Max coughed hard. "I am?"

"Yup. No matter how bad things get with the witches and stuff, I'd take that over the months with no clients any day."

Glancing around to make sure nobody eavesdropped, Max said, "Sorry about that."

"No problem. It's not easy when you don't know if you'll be able to afford to eat each day. I ain't been off the streets long enough to forget. Doubt I'll ever forget." J opened his mouth wide and chomped on the oversized burger.

With Drummond spending the night watching Brenda, Max

had even less to worry about, and he had to admit that J had spoken the truth — working a case, and making money in the process, always made the days better. But he couldn't be sure what to think of this case, or if, indeed, they would be taking it on for a significant amount of time. Or billing.

Perhaps reading his mind, perhaps seeing the tension in his brow, Sandra changed the subject. "Do you think PB's going to get mad at us for constantly asking him to watch your mother?"

"The thought has occurred to me. Don't get me wrong, I'm grateful for his help. In fact, I'm not sure we could keep what little business we have going if he didn't help us out. But it does seem a bit unhealthy."

J's face wrinkled. "Why? They get along. What's the matter with it?"

"Nothing's wrong with it," Sandra said, "but your grandmother doesn't always express herself in the best ways."

Max added, "It's one thing for PB to spend a bunch of time with her, it's something else when it seems like she's his best friend."

"I think she is." J sipped some cola from a straw.

"We'd rather he made friends his own age."

"I don't get what the big deal is. So what if PB's best friend is an old lady? That doesn't make a difference really."

Sandra nodded. "True. But it also means he's destined for heartbreak. Chances are she'll die long before him."

"And?"

"And we want to spare him that pain."

J shook his head in disbelief. "You don't think he's seen friends die before? We both have. ODs, cop shootings, suicides — the streets are rough. We had a friend, Squinty — he needed glasses bad, so he got that nickname — and he got beat up all the time. I don't mean punches and kicks. He got plenty of that, too, but I mean real horrible stuff. Anybody had an urge to do anything bad, they often did it to Squinty. Most times, he couldn't even tell who was messing with him. And when he could — well that meant the cause of his pain wanted him to know. Squinty couldn't do anything about it. We tried to help him, showed him some hiding places, and taught him to dumpster dive after everyone else had already picked through what they wanted. He needed to become invisible. But he didn't listen. Or maybe he didn't want to. He only lasted a week. Cops found him hanging from the rafters of an old tobacco warehouse. PB liked that kid. I did, too. So, yeah, Grandma Porter will die eventually, but PBs going to get a lot more than a few weeks with her. My advice — let PB be PB."

Max shared a look with Sandra. Then: "You're a smart kid. I'm sure your girlfriend appreciates that."

"We broke up."

"Oh. Is that a good thing or a bad thing?"

"Just a thing. And I'm not a kid, anymore."

"You know I didn't mean it like that."

"I do. Because I'm smart, right? Since I'm so smart, why don't you tell me all about the case? Maybe I can help. I am part of the team now."

Sandra said, "You are. We're just not sure yet if there's a haunting at all or if the client might be making it up."

Setting his burger down for the first time, J said, "I don't care if she's an insane ghost, tell me all about it. We haven't had one interesting case since I officially started with you guys."

"Get used to it. We have a lot of jobs that are simple research or things that sound interesting, at first, but are quick to disprove."

"Then explain that part to me. I've got to learn about it all, right?"

With a wipe of his mouth, Max patted J's shoulder and launched into a detailed explanation of the Brenda Byrd case. He left nothing out. Not even the visit from Detective Jorge Osorio. Sandra added her information, too — or lack of it.

"Because that's the weird thing," Max said. "On the surface, every part of this case suggests Brenda is either crazy or lying to us."

"But you believe her," J said.

"I don't know. It's the same with the detective. On the surface, he's investigating a kidnapped girl and suspects Brenda to be the culprit. But scratch a little deeper, and suddenly, it seems there might be more to the story."

To Sandra, J said, "I know you said that you and Drummond didn't see anything, but did you feel anything?"

"That's a good question," she said. "I didn't. But I didn't think to ask Drummond."

J grew quiet. From his scrunched brow, he appeared to be thinking. Max raised an eyebrow at Sandra and she grinned in response. They waited.

At length, J looked up. "Are séances real?"

Sandra leaned her head to the side. "Sort of. I mean, if the medium is the real thing, then a séance can be used to contact the dead. They're highly unreliable, though."

"But since we can't see the ghost — if there is one — then maybe a séance would be a method to attempt a conversation."

Max drummed the table. "See that? I was right. You are a smart kid." To Sandra: "What do you think? Can you do it?"

"A séance? No. I'm not a medium. But I have a few contacts that might be able to recommend one. If those don't pan out, we can ask Irene Beck to point us to somebody. But I'd rather not bother her."

"Good idea. I think she's had enough of us for a while. Okay, then. Tomorrow, you try to set up a séance. J, it's your idea, so you stick with Sandra and get everything prepared. I'll follow up on the Detective Osorio angle."

"How?" Sandra asked.

Max didn't want to say, but he knew there would be no getting around it. Sandra would pester him until she grew angry at his stubbornness. In the end, he would tell her anyway. Might as well get it over with. "I'll have to go straight to the source — Cecily Hull."

# Chapter 8

# SATURDAY

THE MORNING BEGAN with plenty of hustle. Everybody had a job to do for the day, and with any luck, there would be some answers later that night. First thing, Max phoned Brenda to tell her they would take her case and that they needed her in the evening for a séance. She thanked him twelve times before hanging up. After calling Cecily Hull's office, Max got an appointment of sorts — he would be meeting her while she viewed a prospective real estate purchase. Fine by him. Her office always weighed on him under the historical litany of Hull family evils.

Sandra poured coffee for them both while J cleaned up in the bathroom. Scarfing down some scrambled eggs, Max thought about how he would approach the conversation with Hull. He sipped his coffee. Swiping through her phone contacts, Sandra composed a list of the best people to call upon for medium recommendations. Max watched her as he thought.

"We must be the craziest couple ever," he said.

She glanced up with an affectionate smile. "I'm sure there were plenty throughout history to rival us."

"I don't know. Who else would get so excited about such terrible things? I mean, if this pans out the way we want, it means our client is being haunted. And if it doesn't, our client might be involved in a kidnapping or murder. Yet we're both happy."

"I can tell you this much," Drummond said as he slipped through the kitchen wall, "Brenda Byrd isn't faking what she told us."

"Oh?"

"Tossed enough to wreck her bed. All night. Twice she started sleepwalking. And since she had no reason to think you have a ghost on the team to watch her, she wasn't putting on a show for anybody. My money says she's being haunted by something."

Sandra said, "But you didn't see anything?"

"I looked everywhere in her apartment building. Even checked under the foundation. Nothing."

"Did you feel anything? A presence?"

"No. Whatever's causing this, I can't reach it."

"Then it's a good thing we're going ahead with this séance."

"Yeah, you should know that when Brenda got your call this morning, she started dancing. The idea that you'd take her case —well, she called some friend right after to say that she's ecstatic and relieved."

Max said, "We're feeling the same way. Of course, getting money helps, too."

"One more thing," Drummond said. "I checked all over that property for any signs of Detective Osorio's suspicions. But if Brenda has Ashley Cortez stashed away somewhere, she isn't in that building. Nothing about Brenda's apartment suggests she's feeding an extra mouth or anything like that, either."

Checking the time on his phone, Max said, "I've got to get going."

"Where are we off to, partner?"

"I'm off to see Cecily Hull. But I need you to stay with Brenda. Make sure nothing happens to her and that she gets here tonight safely."

Drummond's mouth tightened along with his jaw. "I don't like the idea of you paying a visit to a Hull without backup."

"My visit will be pointless if our client gets possessed."

"Yeah, yeah. You know when I was alive, it was just me most of the time. I never had an agency with a capital *A*, yet somehow I got everything done."

Sandra said, "I'm sure you were quite the superman, but we're mere mortals. J and I have to prepare for the séance, so you're the only other member of the team."

"I said *yeah, yeah.* I'm going to do it. Allow a fella a few moments to gripe about being relegated to babysitting — again." Shaking his head, Drummond vanished.

Finishing her coffee, Sandra said, "That could have gone better."

"It could've gone a lot worse." Max cleaned up from his breakfast and grabbed his laptop. With a kiss on Sandra's cheek, he said, "I'm off. Love you."

Following the directions on his GPS, Max headed on 52 North out of the city and into a forested, less developed area. He exited the highway, drove on a few winding roads, and finally turned onto a gravel road that led to a construction site. A large concrete slab with numerous metal posts sticking into the air outlined what looked like the beginnings of a warehouse. However, Max couldn't see why someone would want a warehouse out here. Limited road access, no trains, no airport — nothing close by to service such a facility. His best guess — whatever Cecily Hull was up to out this way, he didn't want to know about it.

Off to the right he spotted Ms. Hull standing next to a burly man wearing a hardhat. A couple paces back, a young woman dressed to impress her boss stood at the ready, tablet in hand. As Max approached, he saw Cecily snap her fingers and spout of something to the woman. She dutifully tapped on her tablet and responded.

Cecily spotted Max. She smiled, but his skin prickled. "Madeline told me you would be stopping by, and I thought she had made a mistake. She's only been working for me a few weeks."

"Not enough time to break her in?" Max said, nodding to Madeline.

"They do tend to break."

Madeline had some bulk to her, but it looked like muscle. The way she stood — balanced evenly on both feet — suggested she might have some training. Perhaps she was a bodyguard as well as an assistant.

Dismissing the burly man with a wave of her hand, Cecily strolled along the edge of the massive concrete slab — the floor for this large project. "From all our previous meetings, I had assumed you wanted as little to do with me as possible. Yet here you are seeking me out." She paused to lean stiffly toward him. "Perhaps your wife should be jealous."

Max forced a grin even as he shoved back the bile rising in his throat. "I'll make this quick. Don't want to get in the way of your busy schedule."

Gesturing to the site, she said, "What do you think?"

"Of what? Your warehouse?"

"This is not mine. Not yet. It belongs to a gentleman who hopes to acquire a government contract to fill it with whatever they want. But he won't get that contract. I've seen to it. Not that the government needed a push from me. Whomever thought of putting a warehouse out here was ignorant, if I'm being kind."

Max coughed. The idea that they could so easily share an opinion stuck in his throat. "Well, I'm sure you'll have fun crushing his dreams and getting yourself a useless warehouse. I wanted to ask you about —"

"*Useless?* Hardly. For what others want, yes, but for me, I have a great purpose for this building. One I think you will especially appreciate." She gazed across the wide area as if seeing the project already finished before her. "The Hull family is diversifying, developing other revenue streams beyond that provided by our control of magic in the state."

"You don't control much of it anymore."

"Little by little it's coming back to us. Even as we reach out to other income possibilities."

"Wonderful. I'm happy that you'll be screwing the lives of other people not associated with witches and magic. But I'm not here to witness the new Hull direction. I needed to ask —"

"This warehouse is perfectly located for people who want to store things others should never see. The Hull family has acquired and continues to acquire many objects which are better left undisturbed. Rather than let these items float around for one coven or another to discover, I'm going to turn this into a repository for such unwelcome objects. Books, too. All the grimoires and shadow histories. I'll have them here."

Max stared at the empty space and he started seeing her vision, too. But he did not share her exuberance for the idea. No single person should have all the power and certainly not all in one place. But that was a problem for another day.

"Detective Jorge Osorio," Max said with enough force to get Cecily looking away from her grand dream.

With a half-hearted effort, she said, "Should I know that name? Honestly, I have dealt with so many police officers over the years, they start to blur."

"You get arrested often?"

"How amusing. But no, I donate far too much money to their various causes to ever get arrested. Don't you know that's why rich people donate to the police? Myself, my family, if I ever had children, then they would be protected, too. Only the most egregious of crimes cannot be bought off — and even then, it is a bit of a sliding scale."

Max brought out his phone and passed through his photos until he could show her the newspaper picture that included both her and Osorio. He pointed to the detective. "You weren't running the Hull family back then, but you were clearly working for them."

She grinned. "Ah, yes. Like I said, a fundraiser. I would be sent to one or two a month. Representing the Hull family when others couldn't be bothered. But don't make the mistake of thinking I knew your detective. He was probably there out of obligation to his bosses, too."

"Are you really going with *just a coincidence?*"

"Are you really naïve enough to think it's a coincidence? It was bound to happen. I frequented numerous fundraising events. Oftentimes, those events benefited the police department. When they did, the police made a showing, bringing some of their most promising young men and women to prance about in uniform and make everybody feel important. You are an unlicensed detective who has cases that sometimes skirt the edges of legal criminality. Thus, you and I both are in positions to come in contact with various police officers and detectives. It is not a coincidence, then, that I should be in a picture with a gentleman you wish to know more about. It also is not noteworthy."

From a few feet away, Cecily's assistant snickered. Max shot her a look, but she kept her head focused on her tablet.

"Maybe you're right," Max said, "but I've learned to read people quite well, and you're not the poker player you think you are. The way your face reacted at that photo — I'm pretty sure you know Detective Osorio in some greater manner."

A tight scowl flashed across Cecily's face before being tamped back under her stoic control. "Perhaps I do. But I pay your retainer. Answers go from you to me, not the other way around."

"True. But I can't do any jobs for you when I don't know who to trust. And you don't pay me nearly enough for blind trust."

All grew quiet. Madeline looked up from her tablet and inched back a few steps. With narrowed eyes, Cecily stared at Max. He held still, choosing not to lock eyes in a challenge but to wait with forced casualness.

At length, Cecily snapped her fingers at Madeline. "Do you have everything I discussed with the foreman?"

"Yes, ma'am," Madeline said, jumping forward like a soldier at attention.

"Take it over to the gentleman and have him sign it. Then tell him to get everything ready. I should have the building purchased in a few weeks."

"Yes, ma'am."

Cecily waited until the assistant hustled off. "She might last." Cecily strolled towards Max's car. "Come on. You want answers, don't you?"

Feeling like he was her assistant as well, Max hurried to her side.

"Your detective did approach me during the reception to that event — not long before that photo was arranged. I imagine he got in a lot of trouble for talking to me. Bosses rarely like their subordinates to chat with those writing the checks. They want to control the entire situation. It's rather laughable."

"But Detective Osorio ignored that unspoken rule."

"He did."

"Are you going to make me ask for every step of the conversation?"

She shrugged. "We'll see what happens. I'm curious what parts are of interest to you."

"At the moment, any part would do. I can't know what's of interest until I know what he said."

Cecily halted and crossed her arms. Dealing with her was like dealing with a witch. Everything had a price attached. But to Max's surprise, she said, "He asked me how much I knew about my family. He made it clear that he had an academic interest in the occult, particularly magic and witchcraft, and that he believed the Hull family had a deep involvement with such practitioners."

"He's not wrong."

"Still, we try not to advertise that reality."

"What did you say to him?"

"I denied it, of course. Told him that those rumors were spread by jealous and envious people as well as those families that wish to see us harmed. He told me that he knew about several instances in which the Hull family had practiced or paid others to practice occult rites. He couldn't prove any of it, naturally, but between you and me, he hit quite a few on the mark."

Max spotted Madeline heading back toward them. He got the distinct impression that when she arrived, the meeting would be over. Rushing through the conversation in his head, he sought any strand that might glean extra information. "What did he want? Pretty gutsy to say all that to you. Did he try to threaten you? Blackmail you?"

"Nothing so pedestrian. I believe he meant the exchange to put me on notice. He wanted me to know that there was a policeman out there watching me and my family — a man not fooled by our fronts."

"Did he ever contact you again?"

She hesitated. "Not that I recall."

"You don't sound convincing."

"The police visited me after a few of your early cases. Being the face at these fundraisers was as close as they could get into the Hull organization. Now, these officials visit me after every one of your cases they find out about. I need to have Madeline make a note that I want somebody to be a new face for us. I'm tired of dealing with all these political heads. But as it were, if your man was with them at any of these hand-holding sessions where I assure them that magic isn't real and is under control, I don't recall. But remember, back then, you came along and destroyed much of what my relatives had built. And even so, unless Detective Osorio becomes Chief of Police, he'll have a hard time getting anywhere close to me." Looking over her shoulder, she nodded to Madeline. "Time to go. I will say this — he can't touch me, but you're a much easier target. Perhaps the police are starting to see you as the Hull's new face. You should be careful."

Max held back a laugh. "If one more person says that, I might have to listen."

As the two women walked back toward the concrete slab, Max felt more confused than when he came to this meeting. Cecily Hull had provided enough information to muck up the waters and nothing more. Was Osorio a legitimate cop, good at his job, who wanted to uncover the Hull family's illegal activities because he thought they were no better than cultists? Or did he understand that magic was real and that the Hulls presented a more serious threat? How had that shaped him? And more than anything, why did he confront Cecily yet never follow up? For years? Unless he was one of the officers visiting after a Porter Agency case. If so, that only opened up even more questions.

Scratching his chin, he got in the car. Before he could drive away, though, his phone rang. Some weeks, it seemed like that thing never shut up. He glanced at the screen — *Mom*. Of course.

Without barely a *hello*, she launched into him. "I understand that you don't care about me like you do others. I'm your mother and mothers expect to be taken for granted. But your own son."

He glanced at the time. Crap. He was supposed to have picked up PB already.

"I'm driving to you right now. Tell PB to be ready."

"Oh, now you expect us to be on the mark for you when you can't be bothered to show us the courtesy of even a phone call to say you'd be late. I thought the point of a cellphone was that you could call us at any time. Or text. I'm not a dinosaur, you know. I know how to text."

Max drove off, putting his mother on speaker but barely listening as he headed to her apartment.

# Chapter 9

EXTRACTING PB FROM MRS. PORTER'S APARTMENT proved to be a challenge, but after fifteen minutes of apologies and another five of her continuing lecture series on parental responsibility, Max finally had his son in the car and headed home. At first, they stayed quiet, and the silence sounded loud after the harping noise of Max's mother. Winston-Salem drifted under his wheels and Max barely noticed.

Without intending to, he laughed. A moment later, PB joined in. "You're lucky," Max finally said. "I've never seen her lay into you like that."

"I don't show up late."

"You're not driving yet. Though we should start teaching you."

PB shrugged.

"Driving's a big deal. Really changes your life."

"I'm fine with my life the way it is. Besides, I've done okay without driving."

"Yeah, but then you have to rely on somebody like me, and I think we've safely established that I'm going to be late."

"I wasn't the one yelling at you. Didn't bother me. I like Grandma Porter and we had time for another game of chess."

Trying to keep his tone light, Max said, "I'm glad you're not mad, but you should still learn to drive. It gives you freedom. And it'll allow you to make other friends."

"I'm fine with the friends I've got." PB folded his arms as he gazed out the window.

"Aside from my mother, who are your friends? You've never brought anybody home, and you've never gone out for the night with anybody."

"Grandma Porter needs me right now."

Max wanted to reach over, but he knew PB didn't like being touched. "I appreciate that. I do. It's admirable, the way you're helping out. But you are entitled to be a teenager, too. You can go out on a date or hang out with a group of friends or —"

"What are you doing? There's no problem here. I'm fine."

"I'm only trying to be a good parent. Part of that means guiding you to the choices that will give you the best chance for happiness."

"I am happy," PB growled.

"For now. But she's going to die. I don't mean to sound harsh, but that's the truth."

"We're all going to die sometime."

"Yes, but she's old and has a serious disease."

"So, I should be kind to her because she won't be around for long?"

"That's not what I'm saying."

"I don't want to hear it." PB kept his head turned away. "She needs help, and you're too busy for her. I get it. You've got to earn a living. Right? That's what you're doing now — you've got a case."

"I do."

"Then that's it. When we get home, let me shower and change clothes. Then you can take me back. I'll stay with her tonight, too."

"I wasn't asking you to do that."

"And I'm not asking for your permission."

Max silenced his retort before he uttered a sound. He had dealt with PB like this before. No matter what Max said, no matter how he approached the topic, PB would continue to respond with statements designed to purposely avoid the actual conversation — a very teenager thing to do. And if PB did engage, it would be with anger. Max had to hope that PB understood the underlying meaning of what he wanted to say and that PB would think over the talk later.

When they arrived, PB stormed into the house. As Max entered the kitchen, PB grabbed a can of soda and stormed off to his bedroom. Moments later, he stormed into the bathroom and ran the shower. Max wondered if he should carry an umbrella with all the bad weather going on under their roof.

Settling at his kitchen-office desk, he stretched his arms and opened the laptop. A little research would ease some of his tension. The subject this time around: Ashley Cortez.

Like most people born after the turn of the century, like Brenda Byrd and Jorge Osorio, much of Ashley's life had been splashed around the internet. Social media had many ills attached to it, but for researching a person's life, it made matters quite easy. As Max swallowed that thought, he decided that was not a point in social media's favor. Except for people like him.

He pulled up some of Ashley's accounts. She had dabbled on practically every major social media site and a few minor ones, too. To help control the focus, he also looked up Jake Cortez's Facebook page. Being older, Jake spent more time on that site than any other, and as her father, he would insist on being connected to her through the site. At least, Max hoped so. Some parents couldn't be bothered to care about their kids. PB should be happy that he took the time to be concerned.

*Stop it.* Max took a cleansing breath. PB was a teenager. He needed time to grow and space to test his boundaries safely.

"And I need to worry about Ashley right now."

Between father and daughter, Max put together a fairly standard life. No unexpected tragedies. No dangerous illnesses. She was an attractive, young girl who probably had to deal with being underestimated because of her looks. Her grades were nearly perfect, and she had an aptitude for microbiology — which she declared as her major after only one semester at Winston-Salem State University. She did go through a Goth period during her middle years in high school, but that was not unusual. In fact, as he clicked through photo after photo, only a few things stood out.

Jorge Osorio was in a lot of the photos. He was more than a family friend. She referred to him as Uncle Jorge, and while Max did not see any suggestion of impropriety, he filed away the idea as a possibility to watch out for.

Ashley liked to photograph everything in her life, yet not a single photo had Brenda Byrd in it. Not even in the background. If Brenda and Ashley knew each other, it was not a close relationship.

Starting in her Goth days, Ashley began wearing a pendant with a swirling symbol. To most, it would look like an abstract bit of art. Max, however, had seen the symbol many times — in casting circles. Whether or not Ashley knew what she wore was another matter. Max made a note to check with Sandra, but he felt fairly confident the symbol helped protect a witch from blowback when casting a spell.

Last, and best of all, Max found a picture Ashley took when moving into her new apartment — her first. She had a selfie standing under the street sign as well as a wide shot of the building itself, complete with the numbers across the entrance awning — 1033 Junia Avenue.

"You ready?" PB said from the hallway. He was dressed, carried a small bag for clothes, and shouldered his backpack with schoolwork.

Max glanced at the clock. He had been lost in research for close to an hour. "Yeah. Just give me a minute and we can go."

With a huff, PB tossed his bags onto the kitchen table and slumped into a chair. Max ignored the behavior, cleaned up in the bathroom, and grabbed his keys. The return drive to his mother's place threatened to bring all the tensions back. But Max blocked it out. He focused on Ashley Cortez and what he might find at her apartment.

# Chapter 10

AFTER DROPPING PB OFF — after getting cold silence from both PB and Max's mother — the drive to Junia Avenue felt rather pleasant. For fifteen minutes, the quiet in the car was peaceful, tension-free. Nobody threatened Max. Nobody attempted to sway him, either. He simply operated the vehicle and focused on the road.

That pleasure ended as he neared the apartment. Situated several blocks south of Winston-Salem State University and paralleling the main drag of Waughtown Street right off Route 52, Junia Avenue began the residential area of the same neighborhood that Brenda Byrd lived in. While Max had no trouble believing the two women never came in contact — heck, he couldn't identify half the people living on his own block — the chances were high that they had passed one another at the market, on the street, or at Forest Park.

Max found that kind of synchronicity fascinating, even if a bit unsettling. It tied in with the energies of the living world — that thing witches tapped into when they cast their spells. And perhaps it pointed toward what might be threatening Brenda.

Up and down Junia Avenue, starter homes and single-story apartment buildings lined the road. Batches of trees and bushes filled in the spaces between. Max walked up to the building — a place that had once been a large house and was later converted into four apartments. Ashley's sat on the left end.

As he checked around to make sure nobody watched, Max wished for Drummond to be with him. The ghost could unlock the door from the inside. This wasn't the first time Max became aware of how much easier the job could be with his ghost partner around, but it may have been the most exposed time. Cars passed on occasion and twice he heard dogs barking nearby. Best to hurry up.

Bending over the lock, Max pulled out his set of picks and got to work. He had been practicing at home but the techniques which appeared so simple in the YouTube tutorials never quite clicked for him. He understood the concepts, but when he attempted to use them, the practical world had other plans. After a few minutes with Ashley Cortez's door, Max had to admit that he still was not very good at lockpicking.

Instead, he put his hands in his pockets and strolled around the building, hoping to appear casual as if he belonged. Turning the corner, he reached the back of Ashley's apartment. A kitchen door with a window next to it were the only access points. Max had no intention of trying another lock, so he checked the window.

It gave a little. He tried it again, putting in a bit more heft, and the window slid up. With a small grunt, he pulled through the opening and slipped onto the kitchen floor. Hardly the first time he had broken into a home through the window, yet somehow, he always ended up folded on the floor, panting heavily and slightly bruised.

"Enough whining, pal," he said, doing his best Drummond impression. "Get up and check the place over."

With a groan, Max rolled up and stood. The tiny kitchen looked typical for a small apartment — functional without any extra amenities. A stench rose from the trashcan. He guessed Jake Cortez refused to release the apartment but couldn't handle visiting the place, either. Stinky, but good for Max — most likely, nobody had tampered with the rooms since the police left.

His first pass through the place presented a basic one-bedroom apartment fit for a college student who didn't need much and didn't know she could get better for her money. The carpet looked a grade down from the cheap crap at a cheap office, and the numerous wall patches had not been smoothed or painted over properly. The red couch, smashed coffee table, and two toppled chairs remained untouched from when the crime scene photo had been taken. A faint smell of cigarettes masked by tons of incense permeated the air. Her bedroom could only hold a twin bed and a vertical dresser. The bathroom barely held a toilet and tub. The sink had to be situated over the toilet.

Not really horrible living conditions, but nothing special. Max had seen worse. He'd lived in worse.

Ashley's growth from teenager to college student could be seen from one room to the next. Though she had adorned her bedroom walls with Goth posters and covered the window with a dark sheet, the main room had been decorated brighter, more open. Her bookshelf contained plenty of E.O. Wilson, Charles Darwin, and Sigmund Freud. But also Frederick Pohl, David Baldacci, and Brandon Sanderson. An eclectic mix.

Max had no trouble picturing the attack. The struggle by her red couch. Perhaps she threw a book at her assailant. She tried to run for the kitchen, for the back exit, but to no avail. It happened quick. Faster and less violent than depicted in the movies.

Or perhaps she didn't run for the kitchen. She had clearly fought back some. Perhaps she had more fight than most realized. Still, the kitchen was where the knives were. Unless she had something more dangerous in her bedroom.

Max didn't recall Detective Osorio mentioning a gun or other weapon found here. But that didn't mean there wasn't one. A Goth girl with rather straight parents may have learned to hide things quite well.

Entering the bedroom, he patted down the mattress and rifled through the drawers. He checked under the bed and felt the carpeting. Nothing. No false bottoms to the drawers, no stash in the bed, no weak spots on the floor that might be a loose board.

He pulled aside the accordion door to the closet, but it stuck at the end, unable to fold completely open. He leaned his head in and tapped on his phone's flashlight. A portable safe sat on the floor, a bit too big for the door to clear.

With his pulse picking up, Max reached down with one hand and pulled. The safe turned out to be heavy and cumbersome. After two more failed attempts, he had to spring the folding door off its track in order to get a good hold on the safe. Even then, he could only drag it out. Not so portable after all.

Beads of sweat dappled his skin as he surveyed the box. The lock poked out on one side — a keypad for a digital combination. Hard enough to pick a mechanical lock. Max had no skills for figuring out a combination. He'd have to come back with Drummond and have the ghost stick his head inside.

Moving to the other side, intending to drag the safe back into the closet, Max spotted a cutout section of carpet. It had been under the heavy box, probably for a long time, but it clearly had been snipped out from the floor. Staring at it, his heart revving up to a steady pounding, Max leaned closer. He licked his lips.

Pulling the cutout back, he found a sawn piece of wood flooring. He couldn't catch hold of the edges with his finger and had to go to the kitchen for a butter knife. With that, he pried up the small wood panel. A startled breath escaped him as he uncovered Ashley's cache of witchcraft and occult supplies.

Pulling each piece out and lining them up on the floor, Max discovered many of the usual items — various colors of candles, various colors of chalk, long stick matches, as well as several books on Wicca. But he also found several books on occult philosophies which he considered suspect. From all he had learned through Sandra and on his own, many of these books were the paranormal world's equivalent of snake oil salesmen. Then there were the books on crystal therapy and astrology charts. When it came to magic, Ashley's interests spread the full continuum of real to fake to absurd.

Noise from the front door. Somebody fiddling with a key. Crap.

Adrenaline kicked in, and Max rushed to put Ashley's things back in the hidden section of floor. But the narrow opening required great skill in Tetris to get everything to fit. The front door lock clicked. Max grabbed three books and swung toward the hiding spot. One book slipped and clunked across the floor.

The front door started to open — rusty hinges whined but stopped sharp. "Hello?" Detective Jorge Osorio called out.

Max glanced at the fallen book. A pamphlet had dropped out

of its pages. A pamphlet Max had seen before. One promoting the Brotherhood of the Rising. His stomach lurched.

"Hello? Max?" Pushing the door wide open, Osorio's feet clumped as he entered. "I know you're in here. Don't run."

A quick peek down the hall — Max saw Osorio standing in the entranceway. The detective held a gun and a mean glare.

# Chapter 11

HIS HANDS SHOOK. His mouth dried. With jagged motions, Max snatched up the pamphlet, folded it, and stuck it in his back pocket. A quick swallow, a cleared throat, and he said, "Osorio?"

Detective Osorio entered the bedroom, arms stiff as he gripped his gun tight. Seeing Max, his shoulders relaxed and he lowered the weapon. A ripple of nerves shuddered over his body. "You're one lucky fool."

"Most of the time, I can't say it feels that way."

"Today, it's true. You came awfully close to being shot." Osorio patted his sleeve against his brow. "Call came in about a possible break-in at this address."

"And you know exactly whose place it is."

"Of course. I've spent a lot of time searching through this apartment. If I hadn't been there when the call came in, you might've had of very different outcome."

"Then for Ashley's sake, I guess it's a good thing I'm lucky today."

"You found something?" Osorio looked around the room and at Max, putting together what he saw. "The fact that you're here tells me you've looked into the case. You believe me now."

"I never doubted you that Ashley had gone missing and might be in serious danger. Can't say you've convinced me that Brenda Byrd is responsible."

"But you found Ashley's stash. That's just the tip of it. She has other places she hides stuff."

"This only tells me that she was playing around with things she didn't understand. In that way, I suppose she's similar to Brenda. But I'm not getting much more."

Osorio dropped onto the corner of the bed. In a confidential tone, he said, "I see the way you look when you're listening to me. I see how you react to all this spooky magic stuff. Let me tell you something — this stuff is very real to her. And to Brenda Byrd. You understand?"

"Oh, I know about this kind of thing."

If that surprised him, Osorio's face did not betray it. "Then you should hear how she got into this crazy stuff. Because I think it's at the heart of her going missing."

Feeling the Brotherhood pamphlet in his back pocket as if it were a craggy rock pushing into him, Max nodded. "Okay, then. Let's hear it."

Osorio hesitated like an actor waiting on a lighting cue. Except no change occurred. He sat there and waited, and Max wondered what scared the detective so much that he had to summon the courage to continue. Then again, Max knew plenty of things that could petrify a person's senses. He just wasn't sure Osorio had experienced those. Or Ashley — he hoped.

"Until she was a teenager," Osorio said, barely more than a whisper, "Ashley was an incredible, sweet little girl. If you ask Jake, he'll tell you he has no idea when his daughter became so dark. But I know. I know exactly when it happened. See, I was there when she was fifteen, when we all gathered at the Cortez's house to celebrate the Day of the Dead. You know about that?"

"I've seen the movie *Coco*."

Osorio snorted a laugh. "It's no cartoon for us. We take it seriously."

"It's a chance for you to commune with your loved ones who have died. A chance for atonement, redemption, or just remembrance. Is that about right?"

"Close enough. That particular year everything went as it normally did. Now that she was fifteen, Ashley went all out painting up her face in the traditional skeletal look and even wearing a new dress. Everybody was so excited for her. Her quinceañera had been a month earlier and had been a great party. In some ways, this felt like a continuation. We took picture after picture. And the selfies — her and her teenage friends couldn't get enough taking photos of themselves."

"Really?" Max thought over Ashley's social media. Not a single photo of her decked out for the Day of the Dead.

"That was it. The very next day she started wearing all black and dark makeup. Black nail polish, black lipstick. The entire Goth thing."

Though Max suspected the truth, he had to let Osorio unspool it in his own manner. But that didn't mean the man couldn't use a little prodding. "I take it something happened that night."

"I didn't know it at the time. Like the rest that night, I finished my last beer, stumbled home, and went to sleep. But as Ashley's behavior became more and more gloomy, as her parents started to worry, I stepped in as Uncle Jorge to talk with her. It took some persistence, but eventually, she told me that on that night, she learned the Day of the Dead was real. I tried to say that of course it's real, that it's important for us to remember our loved ones, but she cut me off. No, no, Uncle Jorge, you don't understand. She then explained that in the middle of the night, she was awoken by the ghost of her dead grandmother. She wanted to make it extra clear to me that this wasn't a dream or nightmare or her hearing some noises of the house settling and attributing it to something supernatural. She insisted that she saw her actual grandmother. A ghostly figure sitting in the rocking chair in Ashley's childhood bedroom. Rocking back and forth — and the chair moved, according to her. By itself. That's what set her on this road to learning more about the paranormal and the occult and magic spells and all of it. Because once she accepted that what she saw was real —"

"The rest of it might be real, too."

"Exactly." Osorio nudged a black candle with his boot. "I didn't take it too seriously. I didn't take any of this seriously. I thought it was a phase. When she started going to Winston-Salem State University, when she started studying the sciences, it seemed like her interest in these other things drifted away."

"Except it didn't. She just hid it."

"Apparently."

Max looked at all the witchcraft supplies and shook his head.

"I've seen a lot of people get hurt messing with this kind of thing. I'm sorry that she got wrapped up in it."

"There's still a chance for her, though. It's not like she was into prostitution or drugs. I understand that there are groups of people who take this stuff very seriously, but that does not mean that her kidnapping —"

"You don't even know if she was kidnapped."

"You saw the photos. You've seen the living room. A struggle happened in here."

"I saw an apartment made to look like a struggle happened. But if she got as deeply involved in this as you think, she may have simply left on her own. She could have joined a coven."

"A coven? Are you serious? You say that like it's a real thing."

As if he floated right behind Max, Drummond's voice echoed in his head — *get out of there now before you push this guy too hard.* Taking heed, Max walked toward the front door.

"You're leaving?" Osorio followed Max down the hall. "You're just going to let a sweet, innocent girl fall prey to whatever this is all about?"

Whirling back, Max said, "The only reason I'm here is because you said my client was the one responsible. But I haven't found anything to connect Brenda Byrd to Ashley Cortez. There is nothing that these two have in common except for an interest in the supernatural — and that's not enough to accuse Brenda Byrd of kidnapping and murder. I get that you're desperate. Your friend has lost his daughter and is relying on you to save the day. I'm sorry about that. Nothing I can do. Unless you have something you haven't told me."

Osorio's mouth twisted and convulsed as he fought saying the words that cropped up his throat. At length, he muttered a few words in Spanish. Then: "Look, you're going to have to trust me. Trust that as a detective, there's no upside to me lying to you. There's no good that would come out of going down this avenue unless it would deliver results. Especially in a kidnapping case where time is a major factor."

"Not good enough. How do you know that Brenda Byrd is involved in Ashley's disappearance?"

"I have my sources."

"Yeah, see, that's the problem. Everything you've said — all this *trust me* stuff, all this doubt about covens and magic and your disbelief — it's all a lie."

"Watch yourself."

"What's the matter? Afraid I might be onto something? Let me erase the doubt. Your source that you're so scared to tell me about is Cecily Hull." The reaction confirmed what Max already knew. "Without her suggesting you look into Brenda Byrd, you never would have found out about the woman. And this sham of you doubting the paranormal is ridiculous. You got into a lot of trouble talking to Cecily about the occult. You have an unhealthy attitude towards it, and I think it's because you have had an experience that makes you wonder how much of it is true. Perhaps your whole story about Ashley and the Day of the Dead is really about you. Perhaps that's why there are no social media photos of her all dressed up and full of makeup on that day."

Osorio stomped right up to Max and punched him in the jaw. Max tumbled back onto the floor. Sucker-punched, he never had a chance to defend himself.

*I warned you to get out,* Max imagined Drummond saying.

"You want a little truth time, huh?" Osorio spit the words out, his face scrunched tight.

"Not if it's going to be told like that."

"I don't like parasites. People like you who take advantage of people like Ashley. Or even Brenda. Yeah, I'm sure you were happy to take Brenda's money no matter what crazy story she spun for you. Well, if she didn't do it, someone like her did — took advantage of a sweet girl like Ashley. Saw the innocence in Ashley's eyes, saw the confusion and sadness in her appearance, saw the occult books and pendants, and thought that right there was the perfect mark. Feed into her beliefs in the paranormal and bilk her for every dime she has. When that tap went dry, kidnapping and, Lord forbid, murder went onto the table."

"It's not like that."

"I tried to warn you away from all of this. I thought if you knew the kind of person Brenda was, you'd run as fast as you could. But now, I'm not warning you, I'm telling you. This case is over for you. Understand? You tell Brenda Byrd whatever the heck you want, but I don't want to see you around any of this ever again. And as far as Cecily Hull goes — take some hard advice here and leave that woman alone. The Hulls are a lot more than a rich family. Stay away from them."

Gesturing to the door, Osorio waited for Max to stand and leave. Max wanted to perform both actions fast, but his head still whirled from being coldcocked by a man who knew how to throw a punch. With a bit of a wobble, he got to his feet and weaved his way out to his car. The apartment door slammed shut behind him.

When he settled into the driver's seat, he took a few minutes to breathe and clear his head. Of course, he would not turn away from the case. Osorio wanted to paint the Porter Agency as opportunistic frauds, but the way the detective spoke, plus what the research had revealed, suggested that Osorio knew spells and magic existed. He just couldn't accept it. Even as part of him embraced it. Easier to point at the things that scared him, call them fake, and throw a punch.

More than being obstinate or defiant, though, Max had to stay on the case because of the pamphlet he had found. The Brotherhood of the Rising was dangerous. The fact that she found out anything about them did not sit well.

Pulling into the flow of traffic, Max didn't like how these pieces fit together. Even worse — it seemed the best chance the Porters had for making any progress rested in the dubious results of a séance.

# Chapter 12

BY THE TIME Max stepped into his home, his jaw had discolored and the slightest brush against it felt like lemon in a papercut. That didn't surprise him. He had taken a punch more often than he liked to remember. What did surprise him — the house was empty. No Sandra. No J. No séance.

Tented on the kitchen table, he found a note. Apparently, the medium did not like the energies at the Porter home. They needed to hold the séance closer to the source. So, Sandra packed up the supplies, and they drove out to Brenda Byrd's apartment.

Max let out a few choice words as he cleaned up and changed his shirt to one without his blood on it. A simple text would have saved him a lot of time. Ignoring the grumble in his stomach that matched the grumbling he managed on his own, he returned to his car and drove back through the city.

When he finally arrived at Brenda's building, preparations for the séance were in full swing. Sandra stood in the kitchenette with Brenda while J pushed a sofa and chairs to the walls of the main room. Two sticks of incense burned by the sink while Drummond hovered near the corner.

"What happened to you?" Drummond asked when he saw the bruise on Max's face.

"Had a little run-in with a fist." Max kissed Sandra's cheek. Brenda smiled and he realized she had not heard Drummond's question but accepted the answer as his greeting and explanation. He hoped she couldn't read in his expression all the conflicting thoughts he had about her.

Swishing across the kitchen, Drummond said, "Before we get into this, I want it clear between all of us that just because I'm capable of doing a task you all can't do, does not make it my duty. I babysat this gal all night, and it made me long for hanging out in a cemetery. Boring doesn't even cover it."

Talking through Drummond, Max said to the room, "It's been a long day. Perhaps we can get started right away when the medium arrives."

"Mistress Danika is already here," Sandra said. "She's in the bedroom. Has to get her mind clear and receptive. Sorry, hon. Have a seat and wait. I'll pour you some coffee."

Max slumped at the round table situated next to the kitchenette and tried to ignore Drummond's gleeful gloating. He wanted to say something to the ghost, but with Brenda in the room, that conversation would not go well.

When Sandra returned with a steaming mug, Max allowed his brain a moment of calm. He glanced over at Brenda and noticed that she wore a colorful dress displaying her African heritage. She had also put on lipstick and eyeshadow with gentle taste giving him the feeling that he was underdressed for the occasion.

"I want to thank you," she said, her features open and beaming. "Whatever made y'all believe me enough to set up this night, I can't tell you how much it means to me. This kind of thing don't happen normally. I've had my experiences in the past and even my fellow Peepers think I'm fibbing."

Sandra gave Brenda's hand a squeeze. "We're happy to help. Though don't get too excited just yet. We've never done a séance before, but what I do know about them says they're finicky things."

"I don't care if nothing happens at all. It's the fact that you're even trying is what I appreciate. Course I want something to happen. I think. I mean I want to know what's going on with me, you see. But between you, me, and Jesus above, I'm scared what I might find out."

"In my experience, not knowing something is worse. At least, if you know what's haunting you, then you can make a plan to deal with it."

"You sound like my mama. She always said pretending away a pain won't make the pain pretend. You got to deal with the problems in your life. It's not always pleasant, but when you push on through it all, life is usually better on the other side."

Drummond said, "Her mama's a smart woman."

J walked over, gave Max a shuck on the arm, and said to Sandra, "I think we're ready for the table."

Sandra stepped over to the main room to inspect J's work. Max decided there would be no better time to probe Brenda for answers than in her current mood. But the séance would begin soon. Given the lack of time, he opted for the direct approach.

Throwing Drummond a look that said, *Pay attention,* Max crossed his legs and said, "My research into your situation has brought up a name. Does Ashley Cortez mean anything to you?"

Brenda sat straighter. "Can't say I recall that name."

"Maybe you met her in passing? Her interest in the paranormal is what made me think you might know her."

"Now there was a young lady who came to a Peepers meeting not too long ago. Trying us on, you see. Not somebody I wanted to get to know, though. She had a haughty way about her. I mean I understand that the Peepers isn't for everybody, but you don't have to make a scene about it."

"A scene?"

"When she left the meeting, she could've gone home and lived her life and never crossed our paths again. But instead, she got up halfway through and declared that we were too tame for her. Even posted on Facebook about it. Can you imagine? I'm fine that she didn't like the level of magic we were looking at, but to spit on us like that."

"And this was Ashley Cortez?"

She shrugged. "Her name started with an *A,* I remember that. Could've been Ashley. But could've been Angela or Annie or anything."

Sandra and J returned to take the table into the main room. As he lifted, J said, "Are we going to destroy this table, too?"

"Excuse me?" Brenda said.

Drummond snickered. "Kid, you're a pickle."

"Last time," Sandra said, backing toward the hall, "we were casting a spell. This is a séance. It's different."

J said, "But isn't a séance just a fancy group spell?"

"Smart boy," a thick Southern voice said. Mistress Danika.

She waited until the table passed before stepping up to Max with her hand out. She looked like a soccer mom squeezing in the séance before she had to pick up the kids from ballet and piano lessons. As he shook her hand and exchanged pleasantries, he had to remember that Sandra wouldn't have brought in a charlatan. He needed to reel back his presumptions.

Her teeth flashed when she smiled and she moved about with the bouncing energy of a politician or an overeager parent trying to get a seat on the PTA board. "I want to thank you all for having me here tonight. I have been a medium for plenty of years and I've communed with the spirit world more times than I can count, but the opportunity you're presenting me with — I could not turn it down."

"We're happy to have your expertise and assistance," Sandra said.

Max, however, could not hold back a side-eyed look at his wife. To the medium, he said, "What's so special about tonight? We're asking you to do what you've always done."

Mistress Danika forced a giggle as if trying to be entertaining at a party. "Why, dear, you are the Porter Agency. Working with you is a big deal. You stopped the Hull family's domination over North Carolinian magic. That freed up so many opportunities for people. Before all that, it was tough to make a living as a witch when you had to get every move you made approved by the Hulls."

"You're a witch?"

"Not at all. But the service I provide means that I have had to deal with members of the witch community from time to time. Through them, and others, I have come to know your name and the respect it is due. That is why it is my honor to be here tonight." She reached out towards Brenda. "You must be the star of the evening. Come here and give Mistress Danika a hug."

On the edge of blubbering into tears, Brenda embraced the medium. "I do hope you can help me. I don't know how much more of this I can stand."

"Don't you worry. We're going to find out who or what is giving you trouble and fix this up fine. Ain't that right, Mr. Porter?"

"It's Max. And yeah, we'll do our best."

Clutching Brenda's shoulders, Mistress Danika leaned back as if admiring a piece of art. "I do think that you and I could be great friends."

"You're too kind."

"I'm serious. I have a sense for these things. After all, it's my heightened senses that gives me a job."

"In that case, I'm sure I would greatly enjoy your friendship."

Drummond said, "I would greatly enjoy for this night to be over. You know, Miss 1800s has still got a thing for me. I could be in the Other right now enjoying a date."

Max stifled a laugh. Sandra and J were not so polite. From behind their hands, they giggled.

Mistress Danika laughed, too. "Listen to us. Like a couple of schoolgirls. Okay, okay, enough dillydallying. Everyone into the other room."

The group marched into the main room and took up seats at the table. Drummond cut through the wall and hovered a few feet away. With her eyes closed, Mistress Danika spread her arms wide and inhaled the air of the room.

"This space is not quite ready." She raised a quizzical eyebrow. "I'm sensing two strong forces that need to be identified so I do not connect with the wrong target of our inquiry."

Drummond stuck his hands in his coat pockets. "I think she's talking about me."

"There is a ghost here," Sandra said. She then explained about their spectral partner of the Porter Agency.

"A ghost detective? Delightful," Mistress Danika said.

Brenda had a huge smile, but her eyes darted around the room. "Is he dangerous?"

Drummond cocked his head to the side and gazed down at her. "Depends on who you are."

"Not at all," Max said. "At least, not to anybody in this room.

Our enemies have a different experience."

Mistress Danika walked behind J's chair. She put her hands on his shoulders. "I believe I have found the second strong source of energy in this room."

"Me?" J looked toward Max and Sandra for help. Though there was no danger, Max had to admit that it felt good having his son look to him as a parent who could provide salvation from an unfamiliar situation.

"Of course, you," Sandra said. "I've been saying you're special for a long time."

Stepping back to the head of the table, Mistress Danika said, "Very special, indeed. Now that I know the identity of our two forces — Mr. Marshall Drummond and Mr. J Porter — we will find it much easier to isolate the energy we are trying to connect with. Is everybody ready?"

"Are you kidding?" Brenda said. "I can't wait any longer."

Max grinned. "I guess that's true for all of us. Even our ghost detective."

Sitting down, Mistress Danika said, "In that case, I am ready as well. For the journey we are about to embark upon, I am your Captain. I will lead us and you will follow. I will explain everything you need to know. Beyond that, you must trust me." She paused to make eye contact with each member at the table. "Very well. Let us begin."

# Chapter 13

AT MISTRESS DANIKA'S REQUEST, Sandra turned out the lights. Within a single breath of darkness, the playful banter shut like the closing of a book. Somebody's leg bounced vigorously under the table. Though it cast no light upon the rest of the room, Max saw Drummond glowing near the corner. The ghost's face had taken on a sternness that Max knew well — Drummond was not fooling around. He paid close attention. Any sign of threat and he'd be ready to fight.

Mistress Danika struck a long stick match. "A séance is not a spell, and I am no spellcaster. When it works, it does so because we are all open to receiving communications from beyond. We can only achieve this by creating a conducive atmosphere." She lit one of two white candles on the table. "We will succeed or fail together. As a medium, I am merely more attuned to the spirit world. I am a conduit. But I cannot bring about success without your help and co-operation."

As she lit the second candle, Max marveled at how she had transformed from a bubbly soccer mom to a mystical medium. She sounded the same. Looked the same. Yet her demeanor commanded more serious attention. This woman knew exactly what she was doing. Max had seen this unique brand of confidence before. Many times. The confidence of a witch.

"Once we begin," she said, "we do not want to stop until a link is made. So, if you have any questions, this is your last chance."

Raising his hand a tiny bit, Max said, "What should we expect? We got to chant or something?"

Sandra smacked him in the shoulder. "Don't be rude."

"It is a fair question," Mistress Danika said. Max stuck his tongue out at Sandra, and she made a face back. Mistress Danika continued, "Some mediums prefer to use chanting, some require it, but not me. I find it rather distracting and, between y'all and me, a bit hokey. It was a useful technique a century ago, but we're more sophisticated now. As for what to expect once we make contact, that all depends on the spirits themselves. Some will make simple disturbances in the room. Knock on the walls, a closing door, that kind of thing. Others will try to speak through me. And in the strongest connections, there may be a manifestation. No way to tell until we start."

Drummond said, "To be clear, there's still nothing here. Not another ghost on this block, right now, either."

Taking a cleansing breath, Mistress Danika put out her arms and released a sense of comfort across the table. Whether from her demeanor or the incense or something Max could not perceive, he didn't know, but she put the group at ease. They were already becoming receptive for the séance. Without instruction, everybody joined hands. Max, Sandra, and J had all been involved in similar procedures when casting certain spells. And Brenda — she'd read enough about this, no doubt.

"I ask all at the table," Mistress Danika said, her voice pulling everybody in tight like a master storyteller over a campfire, "to relax your bodies and open your minds. Whatever your fears — let them go. Let them be free of you. Open your heart and your soul to accept the true world around you. Share your inner-energy by taking a breath with me and upon releasing it, push that energy out through your fingers and into the hands you hold. With me now."

She inhaled deeply, and Max could hear the entire table inhale as well. When she exhaled, the others did, too. He could feel it. He could feel the energy pushing out from him, as well is that which his body received from the others.

"Again," she said.

The second breath felt stronger than the first. He lightened in his seat. Like a pleasant high, he relaxed, and a euphoric warmth drizzled down.

Mistress Danika lowered her head, letting her hair reach the table. A hum grew from deep in her chest, reverberating in her throat, and exited along with a simple phrase — *welcome here.* The hum began again, rolled up her throat, and this time when she said *welcome here,* she lifted her head. The third time through, she arched her head back saying the words loud and clear, "Welcome here."

Lowering her head, she began the sequence again. Slow and quiet. Building. Growing in power each time through until arching her head back and speaking the words with strength. Max looked to Sandra, but she shrugged. They had quickly departed from familiar witchcraft. This kind of ceremony was new to her, too.

The fifth round through, the lights flickered on and off several times. Mistress Danika stopped mid-phrase. She looked around, perhaps waiting for the lights to flicker again. "A good sign. Remember to be open. We want to receive the spirits, and the more open we are, the easier it is for them to reach us."

Rather than resuming her mantra, she closed her eyes and put her arms out wider — never breaking the circle — trying to open her body. Clearly, she wanted the others to do the same. Sandra was the first, and the rest at the table did their best to follow along.

Swishing to the side, Drummond pointed at the window. "Any of you seeing this?"

Max shook his head.

"There are these whisps of smoke coming through the window." Drummond hunched forward and sniffed the air. "Smell like burnt oil."

"I can feel the spirits," Mistress Danika said. "But they're straining to reach us. They are not like normal ghosts. Something is wrong with them. They are troubled. In pain."

"I'd be in pain, too, if I looked like these fellas." Drummond floated closer to the table. "This one is hanging over everybody."

Max, Sandra, and J all gazed upward as Drummond pointed at Mistress Danika. The medium snapped her head forward, and Max felt heat through his hands. Her eyes turned milky white.

"Samson Price," she said in a masculine voice that stepped

out of a century ago. The words came out slow and gasping. "Help me."

"Another whisp is coming," Drummond said.

Brenda's body stiffened as her eyes milked over. "Been ripped away."

"Sandra, watch out."

Too late. Max watched as Sandra jolted. The color in her eyes clouded over until he only saw an off-white haze. "I am Samson Price. I'm burning."

Max looked to J. "Let go of the circle. Get out of this room."

"No," J said. "I'm not leaving Sandra or anybody."

"I don't want you getting hurt."

"If we break this circle, we might hurt them, right? Besides, I—" His face blanked as a whisp entered into him. "Please, help me."

Bracing to be the final victim, Max winced. Nothing happened. "Drummond?"

"That's all of them," Drummond said. "Of *him*, I should say. We've seen shredded ghosts before, but this — I don't know what it is. It was Samson Price, but he's in four pieces of — I don't know — something."

Swallowing back the urge to shout at everything, Max tried to think. With a shaking breath, he decided to follow the tried-and-true success method of the Porter Agency. "Okay. We started this séance to talk with this thing, find out what it wants, so let's do that." He cleared his throat. "Mr. Price? Can you hear me?"

"Yes," Price said through Brenda.

"How about me? Can you hear another ghost?" Drummond said.

"Yes," Price said through J.

Max didn't want this interview to take long. If any harm came to the living at the table — especially Sandra and J — Max thought it might destroy him.

Drummond said, "Why are you after Ms. Byrd? What do you want from her?"

"Help. I slept. I moved on. Yet I'm here." Each sentence came from a different mouth, but they all shared the same tortured tone.

"You moved on?" Max said. To Drummond: "Is that possible? Can a ghost come back here after they've left?"

"I did."

"But you chose that. Can somebody force a ghost back?"

Opening his hand toward the whisps, Drummond said, "Sure looks that way. But it tore Mr. Price into pieces."

"Who did this to you?" Max asked Mr. Price.

"They want me," Price said. "To use me. I call upon any who can help. Please."

"Listen to me. We want to help. If somebody pulled you from beyond, is trying to use you for a spell, then they have to control you."

Drummond snapped his fingers. "That's right. These whisps must only be the part of him that can get free. Mr. Price, look around you. There should be a summoning circle or some type of spell. What do you see?"

Price said, "Dark. Murky. Liquid. Oh, the poor dear."

"Concentrate," Max said. "We can't help you unless we can find you. Where are you?"

All became quiet. A breath. Another. Then: "I think — a warehouse."

"Good, good," Drummond said. "Is it an old building or new?"

"I hurt everywhere. Let me go. Let me get back."

"Come on, now, Mr. Price. You want to be free? You want to move on again? You've got to give us something we can use."

Another moment of quiet. Then: "Broken windows."

"An old warehouse?" Max said. "Can you see out the windows? Can you tell us what's out there?"

"Barbed-wire fence. Weeds. A street."

"Good. Good." Drummond spoke fast as if he knew they had little time left. "An old, abandoned warehouse. What else? Street name? Train tracks?"

"A white wall with bits of brown paint half-done. This isn't another war, is it? I don't see flags or banners or any of that crap they're always decorating everything with. I'm still in America, ain't I? Please. Hurry. I can't take it anymore. Please."

Sandra and J dropped their chins to chests. Brenda's head lolled back, and Mistress Danika flopped forward, smacking her forehead on the table. Max could see the milky haze in their eyes had vanished.

"Is he still here?" Max asked Drummond.

But when he looked up at the ghost, he saw Drummond staring out the window. A bright light shined on his pale face, but the light came from no source Max could see. He could feel it, though. Not warmth. Not sunlight. But peace. An overwhelming sense of joyful peace as if his heart swelled with falling in love, with dropping into the comfort of kind arms, with the concerns of the world fluttering away. Max couldn't be sure, but he swore he saw a tear on Drummond's cheek.

"Everyone okay?" Mistress Danika said as she sat up.

The light snapped off Drummond, and he turned to the group. He kept his head low for a moment, and rubbed his face. When he finally lifted his gaze, he appeared as always.

The rest of the group looked shaken but unharmed. Though J stayed quiet, he sat a bit taller. Brenda jumped to her feet and rushed over to the medium.

"Thank you," she said, clearly wanting to hug Mistress Danika but managing to hold back. "Thank you so much." She cried. "I knew I wasn't crazy."

"It seems you have a ghost who wants your help. That's good. Better than wanting to harm you."

"Thank you, truly. It's wonderful. So, what do we do now?"

Mistress Danika gathered her things. "Not *we*. You. And the Porters, of course. They're more than capable. I'm just the person who makes the connections. I have no skill beyond that." She paused and took Brenda's hand. "I do hope you'll call me when this is over. We could have tea and you can tell me all about what happens."

Sandra walked with the medium to the door. "You've done more than enough."

"More than you expected, I'm sure. Don't worry. No offense taken."

"Good, because I imagine we'll be using your services again someday."

Mistress Danika glanced at the séance table. "I'd rather not. This was, well —"

"More than you expected?"

"I suppose so. I'll email you the bill. It was a pleasure meeting y'all, but I think I'll stick to helping people reach out to their loved ones from now on."

Max hadn't noticed until that moment, but the woman's hands trembled. Her eyes darted around the room, and every time her gaze fell upon the table, a shiver rushed over her. When she left, they heard her staunch a terrified cry in the hallway.

Brenda turned to Max. "You heard what Mistress Danika said. You're the ones who can help me, help this ghost, and put an end to all of this. I mean, you have to believe me now."

"We do. And don't worry. We'll take care of this."

"Then what do we do?"

It was a good question. Max looked at Sandra, then J, then Drummond. They all took a second to think.

Drummond spoke first. "Seems obvious to me — we've got a warehouse to find."

# Chapter 14

THEY HELPED CLEAN UP the apartment before driving home. The late-night air smelled of a rainstorm, but when they entered the house, Max thought about setting up on the front porch. It was small out there, barely an awning to protect him, but as long as the storm wasn't too heavy, he thought he'd be okay. Besides, he had tired of working in the kitchen office. That tiny alcove hardly created an atmosphere conducive to long, intense research, and if he had learned anything through the séance, he learned that a proper atmosphere meant everything.

J shuffled toward his bedroom. As excited as he had been throughout the night, the adrenaline crash hit hard. He would be asleep in minutes.

Watching him blunder off, Sandra smirked. "I can't think of the last time I've seen him so worn out."

"Probably Carrowinds," Max said. "He seemed invincible standing in line for one rollercoaster after another. But I remember getting home, looking in the back seat and both him and PB were out cold."

With a clap of his hands that startled both husband and wife, Drummond appeared near the side door. "I think we're in good shape. Never thought a séance would produce real results, but I guess even I can be wrong once or twice."

"Or more," Max said.

"I'm choosing to ignore that because we've got work to do. Samson Price is out there in a warehouse, and he needs our help. We do that and our client should be free of her haunting. So, how do you both want to play this?"

Sandra said, "I'll send an email tonight to my old real estate contacts. Shouldn't take long to have a list of possible warehouses. Especially since the ghost — or pieces of ghost — said that the place looked abandoned. Either it's on the market or a lot of agents would like it to be. They'll know about it. After that, I'm going to sleep. I can barely keep my eyes open."

With a peck on the cheek, Max said, "I'm going to research Samson Price. The more we know about him, the better. Might help us narrow down the list you get tomorrow. I'm guessing it'll be long."

"Why? There can't be that many abandoned warehouses in the city."

"He could be anywhere in the state. Maybe even South Carolina or Virginia."

"No," Drummond said. "Split in four pieces like that — I doubt he's very far. Those bits of smoke that I saw of him stretched out the window almost like a tether. And the pain he was in. I'm guessing that whatever curse or spell brought him back also keeps him locked in that warehouse. He's only got so much range before the pain is too great."

"We won't know until we get cracking on it."

Winking at Drummond, Sandra clapped her hands together once. "Well, you boys have fun chatting about it. I'm going to write that email and get to sleep. Good night." With that, she left the kitchen.

"No real chatting to do," Drummond said. "I'll go back to Brenda's place and hoof it around the block and a few surrounding blocks. See if he's closer than we realize."

"Wait," Max said before the ghost could disappear. "I want to ask you something."

"Yeah?"

Drummond hovered, and something in the way he held himself, in the slight downward indent in his brow, in the sensation of cold wafting off his ghostly body — something about it all sent warnings through Max's chest. Instincts fled, and Max struggled with whether to ask his question or bury it. But to drive it down in his soul, to ignore what he had seen — what he had felt — did not seem feasible. It would have been easier to hide the discovery of cold fusion or time travel.

"During the séance," Max finally blurted out. "I saw — you."

"Yeah, I saw you, too. I think we all saw each other."

He could see it on Drummond's face. The ghost knew what was coming but refused to make it easy. Max said, "That light." The words nearly brought tears. "Was that — I mean, was that really —"

"Heaven? No." Drummond shrugged before motioning as if he smoked a cigarette. "I suppose if you believe in that stuff, then you might see it that way. But really, it's just the gateway to moving on."

"It felt so special."

"That's on purpose. It calls you. Makes it hard to stay here. For some."

Stepping closer, trying to ignore the deepening cold around his partner, Max went on, "I've never experienced that before."

"You're not meant to until you're dead."

"You know what I mean."

"Yeah. But the fact that it's open, trying to pull Price back in and can't, that's really bad."

"It was incredible. And you've come back from that. How? Why? As much as we love having you here, as much as we need you in these cases we do, I don't see how you can turn away from that."

"It's not all that great."

"I hate to think that we're the cause of you denying some form of paradise."

Drummond's hand flashed out so fast that it took Max several seconds to understand that the icy sting on his cheek came from being slapped by a ghost. He stumbled back a step. Rising toward the ceiling, Drummond's face flared as he jabbed a finger at Max.

"The only reason you're still standing is because I value my partners. So, you listen up. We're not going to have this conversation more than once. I've been alive, dead, cursed, bound, tethered, and freed. I've been to the Other and I've been to what awaits us when we move on. I've even been to a few realms I don't want to think about. None of those experiences were a direct result of you. My life, my choices, are not about you. Just because I care about you and Sandra and the boys, doesn't mean I make existence-altering decisions based on you. The fact that you stand there suggesting your influence on me is that great, suggesting that I could not possibly have made the steps I've made on my own, is more than insulting. It borders on a betrayal of friendship. But I'm going to show you a greater courtesy than you have shown me. I'm going to chalk up your stupidity to the fact that you were mesmerized by that light and haven't been thinking clearly since. I'm going to forget this. I'm also going to leave now. Do me a favor — while you get lost in your research, find a little time to get your head right. I'll see you in the morning."

With that, Drummond vanished.

Max stood in the empty room, unable to respond. A shiver began on the back of his neck and spread like a cold front across the plains. Soon, his entire body shook. He reached out for the counter, missed, and wilted onto the floor. Another moment drifted by before he could gasp for air.

He had seen Drummond lash out before — in frustration, usually. He had seen the ghost fierce — to protect those he loved. But to witness such anger — that was new. Anger came from fear, and without a doubt, Drummond wanted to shut down any possibility of having the conversation go further, deeper. The question, of course — what exactly did he fear?

But no. Max knew he should stop this line of thinking. Not only because Drummond had made it clear he did not want to pursue the matter, but because Max did not exist in that part of Drummond's world. He wanted the ghost to be happy, yet he had no way to accurately research what he had seen. Any searches into ethereal light would bring up religious views, psychic views, witch views — and not a single one would be authoritative. They would all be each person's best guess or desire. Might as well research patterns in winning lottery numbers.

Rubbing his face and neck, he tried to clear the tension. Nothing he could do. No taking it back, and no moving it forward. Perhaps it would be best to do as Drummond had demanded — forget the whole thing. Grabbing a loose tooth from the back of a shark's mouth would be easier, but he could try. For Drummond's sake.

While researching mystical afterlife lighting sources would be impossible, Max could research Samson Price with an excellent chance of success. The work would clear away all these other thoughts — get his mind *right* — plus, he needed to do it. It was his job.

Outside, the rain had slackened off to a drizzle, so Max sat under the front stoop awning and enjoyed the fresh smells of the wet night air. The steady chirp of crickets sang free. Even with the city so near, the quiet of the night surrounded him. Quiet, yet filled with noises of insects and frogs and the occasional dog. Filled with life.

He rested his head on the doorjamb. The world had changed so drastically. A few years back, the idea of partaking in a séance would have seemed ludicrous, yet the moments of grounded simplicity remained. No matter how chaotic things became, many of the true pleasures stood fast — a morning cup of coffee, a loving hug from his wife, a quiet evening. And the joys of research. Nothing could take that from him. He woke up his laptop, and in seconds, his thoughts plunged into the problem at hand — Samson Price.

He started in the most basic fashion. He googled the name. A law office, a dentist, and a sanitation service all came up. Scrolling through the unending pages, there were several million results, Max did not spot a single headline that called for a closer look.

He then turned his attention to social media. As expected, plugging the name into the biggest sites produced hundreds of people named Samson Price. Max used a webscraper to export the data into a usable spreadsheet. From there he started sorting. He removed anybody still alive — knocking the number back to a manageable twenty-five. From there, he cut anybody who, when they were alive, resided beyond North Carolina or the surrounding states. That brought the number down to four.

The first he crossed off the list because the man had died only four days ago. The second and third were removed because they were missing but not officially dead. Max put their information in a new file in case he needed to return them to consideration later. The last Samson Price had been the subject of a publicized exorcism, which according to both the priests conducting the rite and the family plagued by the presence, was a success.

If the man could not be found on social media, that suggested an older ghost. But how much older? He could be from the 1970s or the 1770s.

"Hold on," Max said, sitting straighter as an idea sparked. During the séance, Price mentioned seeing barbed wire out the warehouse window, and he thought it might be wartime. The first use of barbed wire occurred in the late-1880s. While the US had been involved in numerous wars since that time, Price uttered a few other clues. He mentioned not seeing flags or bunting or decorations, and that brought him to question if he might still be in America.

"So, he thought the enemy was one that reveled in pageantry."

Not Vietnam, then. Or the Korean war. The most obvious that came to mind was World War II. The Germans made a big show wherever they went. Like Price had said — flags and banners.

At the least, this gave Max a direction to pursue. He went on the government website archiving all the census data. Searching for Samson Price of North Carolina brought up numerous results that would require a lot of time to go through — the census pages had yet to be digitized. Too many results and too much time.

But Max had that special ripple of excitement through his belly. The answer waited for him in all that data. He merely had to figure out how to find it.

Setting the laptop aside, he gazed down the wet street. A worn Ford Escort rolled along, stopped four houses up and idled. The glow of the driver's phone outlined his face — middle-aged man, glasses, tired. The door to the house opened and a haggard man in a rumpled suit stepped out. He carried a suitcase in one hand

and a briefcase in the other. His wife kissed him and reminded him to wear a mask. The driver got out to help the man with his bags, and Max heard echoes of low-voiced conversation — enough to put the final details. The driver worked for Uber or Lyft or some other such service, and the man needed to go all the way to the big airport in Charlotte — about an hour-and-a-half trip.

As the car drove off, as the street returned to its peaceful noisy-quiet, Max thought about how reliant each person in the city was upon the other. Even two people like these who probably had never met before and would probably never meet again. Like the complexity of the living human body, the citizens of a city were interconnected.

*The dead, too.*

In his experience, ghosts did not hang around just any old place. Those that stayed here or in the Other did so with reason. They were connected to a particular area. Never had Max encountered a ghost from California haunting a home in North Carolina. In fact, he had never encountered any ghost that did not hold some strong link to the city.

What was Samson Price's link? Not only to the city, but to Brenda Byrd as well. Whoever had ripped Price back to being a ghost, whatever magic had spliced him into pieces, could not keep him from seeking help. Yet when given the opportunity, he centered his efforts on Brenda. Not a medium. Not a psychic. Not a ghost-seeing researcher doubling as a private detective. Rather, he strained and struggled and endured whatever suffering he felt to connect with Brenda — a woman who was probably born long after he had died.

One answer came fast, and Max's research instincts told him it had to be right. At least, it had to be the answer with the best shot at being right. Brenda Byrd had to be related to Samson Price.

# Chapter 15

## SUNDAY

WITH BARELY ENOUGH SLEEP to keep moving and barely enough coffee to function, Max meandered through the regular morning routines, even when nobody predicted the day would be regular. Sandra's real estate friends came through with a half-dozen contenders, so they had a clear plan to forge ahead.

Sandra suggested that J stay with Grandma Porter. Max agreed. Not surprisingly, J objected. But PB needed a rest and Mrs. Porter needed to be watched over.

"You wanted to be part of this team," Max said. "Sometimes that means doing the less exciting work so that the team can get the job done."

"Then you go watch her," J said.

"I have. And I will again. But today, it's your turn. Besides, I know you like spending time with her. Not as much as PB, but it's not going to be a hardship."

J grumbled some more, but in the end, he stuffed his backpack with a book and his laptop, got in the car, and ceased any further argument. When they dropped him off at Mrs. Porter's apartment, PB had already left.

"Went for a walk," Mrs. Porter said. "He promised to be back in the evening."

Perhaps reading Max's body language, J said, "Don't worry. PB can take care of himself, and I'll talk with him when gets back. Y'know — brother to brother."

Max had no idea how to take any of that, but they had a warehouse to find. The family issues could wait until PB returned. Patting J on the back, Max kissed his mother and went to the car.

By the time he and Sandra pulled out of the parking lot, Drummond had joined them. Floating in the backseat, he said, "No luck last night. If there's a warehouse matching Price's description within walkable blocks of Brenda's apartment, it must be an invisible ghost, too. When I turned up empty there, I went into the Other."

"Oh?" Max said, checking his partner in the rearview mirror. "Your contacts know anything about him?"

"No. Perhaps. I didn't ask."

"Then what? Is part of Price in the Other, too?"

Sandra glanced back at Drummond and laughed. To Max: "He didn't ask anybody or do anything on the case in the Other. Who was it this time? Miss 1800s again?"

If a ghost could blush, Drummond would have turned a few shades redder. "If I go to that gal too often, she'll start getting ideas. And death is forever, so I have to be careful about that. I did meet a nice curly-haired lady from close to my time. 1952. A little young, but she was a diner waitress and still likes to wear the uniform."

Max gave his head a shake, hoping to dislodge the images Drummond had created. "Can we focus on the case? Please."

"Sounds good to me. How long until we reach the first warehouse?"

Sandra said, "Coming up on the right."

They all craned their heads to where Sandra pointed. Although empty, the building did not look like the ruins Price had implied. No broken windows. No barbed wire. No white/brown wall across the street. Only empty and for sale. Sandra crossed it off the list, plugged the next address into her phone, and directed Max toward the location.

"What about you, partner?" Drummond said. "What did you find on Price?"

"After some wrong turns, I finally realized there was a good chance he was related to Brenda."

"Makes sense. Ghosts don't usually haunt at random."

"I worked backwards starting with her, building a family tree as if I were doing an ancestry for a client. That's when I found him. A little bit about him, anyway. He was very private and kept much of his life out of the public record."

Sandra said, "I know you like to be dramatic about telling us information — turn left at the light — but could you give us some specifics before lunch?"

"Cute. Maybe I'll string you both along and never reveal anything."

"Doubly-cute. Do that, and I'll do the same with our romantic life."

"Okay, you win."

"Not much of a fight."

"You want to gloat or do you want to know who Samson Price was?"

Drummond said, "I thought we were concerned about focusing on the case."

"Okay, okay. Samson Price lived from 1890 to 1942. He was born in Winston-Salem, one of five brothers, and spent much of his life here. He married Edna Byrd. She was sister to Brenda's great-grandfather Robert Byrd. Price worked as a miner. Started out west, originally, but then moved back to North Carolina when one of his brothers grew ill. But here's the thing — that's mostly it. There's nothing in the limited information I could find on him that suggests any connection to witches or magic. He died young, hit by a car, but otherwise, his life was normal. Bland, even."

They arrived at the second warehouse.

At first glance, this appeared more promising. Cracked pavement with weeds poking though covered the small parking lot as if it were a parched desert. The building — hand-hewn brick laid over a century ago — stood like a historical monument more than an active warehouse. Several of the windows had been broken.

But the outside did not match Price's description. Max drove around the entire block looking for the white wall with bits of brown paint. They tested a few odd angles thinking that perhaps in the right light and the right viewpoint, one of the surrounding buildings would take on the necessary characteristics. At length, they decided to mark the address as a *maybe* and move on to the next.

After getting Max on the right road, Sandra said, "I suppose Brenda is in the clear about Ashley Cortez."

"You think so?" Max said.

"She was telling the truth about being haunted. It's hard to believe that somebody going through that experience would have the time and mentality to focus on kidnapping a person."

"Osorio seems to think Ashley was taken because of her occult interests. Maybe for some kind of spell."

"Sacrificing a life is the kind of blood magic used to curse a person or worse. But if Brenda was involved in casting a spell, I think she would have sought to get rid of her haunting."

Drummond tapped his chin. "I agree with Sandra. Don't go thinking this detective will see it that way, though. He's got his brain twisted up into this Cortez case, and when that happens to a cop, it can get real hard not to see suspicious things everywhere you look."

"Even if your suspect isn't being suspicious at all?"

"Especially then. Making it even worse on him is that I'm pretty sure he's working off the books on this one. Far off the books."

Sandra pointed out a turn, and as Max duly followed her instructions, he said, "Because of the witchcraft stuff?"

"That's definitely part of it. He's not going to risk his job going up against Cecily Hull for nothing, and he's not going to risk it going up against his bosses for Cecily Hull."

"Trapped either way he goes," Sandra said.

"Best thing he could do is work the case on his own. He figures if he's lucky, he'll save the girl, which makes his bosses happy and handles whatever occult side of things needs handling which makes Cecily Hull happy. Most important to him, he satisfies that itch — at least, for a little while. But I've seen it before. He's already stepped into our world a bit, and even if he can't accept it completely yet, he's questioning everything around him. Won't be long."

Max said, "What do you mean you've *seen it before?* You talking about yourself? Because that's not exactly the story you told us."

"Sheesh, you are getting paranoid. You really think I lied to you about all that?"

"No, of course not. I didn't mean it like that."

"For somebody so careful in his research, you sure are fast with your mouth. Maybe slow down and think a bit before you speak."

Opening his mouth to respond, Max stopped when Sandra put her hand on his arm. Drummond snickered. "Doll, you'll always be the brains of this operation."

"Thanks. It would help right now if you explain about that comment, though. Who have you seen go through what Detective Osorio is going through?"

"My old partner — Detective Cooper. I'm sure I've told you about him before."

"Some, but not a lot."

A wave of cold swelled throughout the car. It might have been Drummond's unease, but Max couldn't be certain. The car's climate controls acted up on occasion. Perhaps the air-conditioning simply decided to chill the interior for a while. If he simply checked the mirror again, he could figure out the answer by the look on Drummond's face, but a sense of old-time decency kept his eyes on the road.

At length, Drummond said, "Cooper and I started out together as beat cops. You've got to know that much. Then I had my first experience with a ghost, and unlike Osorio, I couldn't pretend it didn't happen. I quit the job and started my own Private Investigator service doing what we're all doing with The Porter Agency. Cooper went on to become a detective. He's more like Osorio — or I suppose, really, Osorio is more like him. See, just because I was no longer a cop, didn't mean cases stopped coming along that involved witches and such. Yeah, I had hung out my shingle, but that didn't mean people knew or trusted me. Even after I became a known figure in the witch community, there were still plenty of cases that found their way towards the police — and over time, those would somehow drift along until they sat on Cooper's desk."

Max said, "I take it your ol' pal didn't like that much."

"Not in the least. Most of the time, he'd sneak those cases off the books and take them to me. He was a good man who wanted to help people and keep the city safe. That meant he couldn't do what the other detectives did — pretend the cases hadn't happened. But he couldn't pursue most of the situations without jeopardizing his career. He had the one advantage, though — me. If any other cop was seen entering my office or having lunch with me or anything, that would get the rumor mill grinding away. But Cooper was my old partner. We had a friendship that everybody knew about long before the weird cases started getting dealt with. I'm sure plenty of the other guys understood what was going on — that's why those cases ended up with Cooper in the first place. They were just well-practiced at not seeing what they couldn't handle seeing."

"You think it's the same now?" Sandra said.

"Don't you? The higher you go up the ladder and the closer you get to hobnobbing with people like Cecily Hull — I'm guessing those men and women have seen a lot more bizarre things that they can't explain, yet they still find ways to deny it all."

Max said, "Cecily Hull told me the cops meet with her after most of our cases."

"Of course, they do. Anything weird happens they want assurances, ways of continuing to pretend. Probably visit her after everything — not just our cases. They've got to put something reasonable in their reports, after all, and everyday shoe-leather detectives won't be signing away their livelihoods over a few spooky bumps in the night. Point is, back in my day wasn't any different. Cooper found himself stuck between two powerful boulders — the world as most people knew it and the world beyond. He'd bring me the bizarre cases and be afraid to follow up on the outcomes. But each new case brought him closer to dealing with the reality of magic."

"This is all very interesting," Max said without sarcasm, "and

I'm truly grateful to learn more about you, but how exactly does this help us?"

Sandra said, "He's building up to something. Give the man a chance."

"It's okay," Drummond said, though his brow knitted tight as he gazed out the window. "I'm almost done. See, nothing changed for Cooper the entire time I knew him. But after that witch killed me and cast her curse that bound me to my office, that's when things happened. Cooper kept showing up and sitting in the empty room. He'd talk to me. It wasn't the way people might talk to a dead loved one as a way of dealing with their loss. He talked to me because he knew it was possible that I was listening. That's what drove him over. While I was around, he could deny everything no matter what twisted logic he had to contort in order to make it all palatable. Oh, he would tell me he started to believe, but a week later, it was all smoke and mirrors again to him. But when I died, that made it click into place. It disturbed him. He knew the Hull family was connected to my death, but he couldn't prove it. The whole thing started eating away at him. He ended up losing his job because he wouldn't stay off of it all. In the end — well, I don't like to talk about that, much less think about it. Let's leave it with the fact that it wasn't a glorious finish to his life. You understand now?"

Sandra nodded. "Detective Osorio is like Cooper. He tries to deny it but something happened or will happen that'll click it together for him."

"He can't let it go. If he's not careful, he'll get fired — at best. He keeps at it, he might end up dead, cursed, or worse. That's bad enough for him, but I'm worried that he'll end up taking the both of you down with him."

Those last words hung in the car. When Sandra pointed out the final turn, Max flinched. They rolled down a road no more than a handful of blocks from Brenda Byrd's home.

"Strange," Drummond said. "I swore I checked all the buildings near her apartment, but I didn't see this one."

"A spell?" Max asked.

Nobody needed an answer.

Ahead, an old warehouse came into view on the left. A long row of windows lined the side — each one cracked or broken. Barbed-wire fence surrounded the property, and on the opposite side of the road, a long white wall stretched the entire length. Small patches of the wall had brown paint where somebody had planned to change the wall's color and stopped early on in the process.

Max parked. They stepped out and stared at the warehouse like a group of strange tourists focusing on abandoned buildings. He knew both Sandra and Drummond looked for any ghosts or signs of witchcraft not visible to others. For his part, Max sought any hint of a casting circle, salt along the doors or windows, or even an occult symbol painted on the jambs.

"I got nothing," he said after a minute.

"Looks clean to me," Sandra said.

"Not quite." Drummond floated across the street at an angle toward the building. He slid through the fencing and around the back. When he returned, he said, "Detective Jorge Osorio is here spying on the place. He's in the back corner on the inside of the fence. There's a gap about halfway along. Must have come from a block over and walked through the tree line bordering that side. Question is: how did he end up at this warehouse, too?"

# Chapter 16

MAX REACHED INTO HIS POCKET — no gun. Stupid. With all the juggling of events in the last few days, he completely forgot about it. Left it in the glovebox. Perhaps it was better that he forgot the weapon. Though he had signed up for target practice, that didn't happen for another week. No bullets in it, anyway. And with a man like Osorio — a man who had been trained to use a handgun, at the least — Max thought his odds of surviving that kind of exchange extremely dim.

Following Drummond's lead, Max and Sandra skirted around the building, using the side opposite Osorio, so that they could reach the gap in the fence without alerting him. Throughout the short trip, Max kept one eye on the warehouse. Lots of graffiti, but nothing suggesting witchcraft or the occult.

"When we get there," Drummond said, floating backwards so he could level his most serious look upon them, "don't move fast or suspicious. This guy's a cop, but he's also acting twitchy. Remember everything I told you about Cooper."

Sandra said, "You think he's unstable?"

"I think I care about the two of you a lot more than I do about him. If I need to freeze his head clean off, I'll do it. But let's not run things up to that point. All I'm asking, doll, is that you be your charming self. And, Max, don't be yourself."

Before Max could throw back a whispered response, Drummond indicated the gap as he swished through the fence. Sandra shot a glance over her shoulder — partly warning Max to stay quiet, partly amused at his expense, and fully loving him. His chest swelled. That she could pack so much into one expression floored him, momentarily swept him away from the warehouse and into a cloud of romantic warmth.

When he ducked through the gap and crouched next to her, he kissed her cheek. "I love you."

She winked and pointed toward a stack of crates in the back corner. Osorio hid behind them, trying to stay out of view of the warehouse windows. But from Max's angle, the detective could be seen quite clearly.

When it became evident that they had spotted him, Osorio leapt to his feet and manically waved them over. Though making himself perfectly visible and an easy target, he did not appear to see the irony as he shouted, "Get over here. Take cover."

Max and Sandra crouched further and scurried behind the crates to join the man. Sweat dribbled down the side of his face, and his unblinking eyes remained locked on the warehouse. His fingers tapped rapidly against the side of the crate.

Max said, "Are you okay?"

"What are you doing here? I warned you off all of this."

"Yeah, it didn't stick. Now what's got you so spooked?"

"The both of you need to go. Get out of here."

"Sorry. Not going to happen."

Sandra said, "Guess we'll have to go in alone."

"No." Osorio wiped at his face. "Somebody moved in there. Saw it only once, but I know it happened."

"Let's go see," Max said.

"Are you crazy? Do you know what might be in there?"

Staying off to the side, Drummond said, "It's like I told you — he's trapped. He's frozen by what he thinks might be in there and what he's told himself can't possibly be true. It's amazing he made it out this far, but he's too scared at what he could find to take those final steps."

Osorio's jittering eyes gave proof to Drummond's words. Max didn't want an unstable situation made even worse, and he knew Sandra would want to help the detective, anyway. Opting for a practical approach, he said, "Brenda Byrd didn't do anything wrong. She certainly didn't kidnap Ashley Cortez. Didn't even know the girl. But someone is causing Brenda a lot of trouble. We don't want her ending up like Ashley or worse. So, we need to know what's inside that warehouse. We're going in."

"You can't," Osorio said, clutching Max by the arm.

In a soft yet authoritative tone, Sandra said, "Let go of my husband." She glared at Osorio until he obeyed. Then: "Max is right in what he said. Our investigation has led us to this warehouse. That's why we came. But you need to explain what you're doing here."

Pointing at Osorio, Max said, "Hey, yeah. Why are you here?"

Shifting around to set his back against the crates, Osorio blotted his brow with his sleeve. "Because of you guys. Because when I found you poking around Ashley's apartment, that got me thinking. I went back there and started searching through the place again like I'd never been there before."

"I've got to hand it to the man," Drummond said. "I have my doubts about him, but he's more of a detective than I gave him credit for."

Osorio peeked back over the edge of the crates as if the warehouse might get up and escape while he wasn't looking. "I went through every inch of that apartment. I had to have missed something. You both have been so adamant about your client, and I admittedly have been going after Brenda on very thin evidence. It's all I had. I can't give up on Ashley. Not ever. Not for her. Not for her father. Not when the slimmest sliver of a chance exists that I might help her."

Sandra said, "No one's asking you to stop."

"After I'd gone through every room and turned up nothing, I decided to do a more desperate search — I pulled out every book on her bookshelf and leafed through the pages. People hide stuff in books, but usually it's cash or a dirty picture or something like that. Sometimes they use a receipt for a bookmark or another piece of paper that can clue us into aspects of their lives."

Feeling a twist in his gut, Max said, "You found something that brought you here."

"That I did. Ever heard of the Brotherhood of the Rising?"

That twisting turned into a full-on punch. "Yeah."

"I found four pamphlets for them. Basic *join our cult* crap that reaches out for people feeling lost or hopeless. Each pamphlet had a different address. I checked out all the places, and every single one took me to an abandoned building of one kind or another. But they were all empty as far as I could tell. Except this one. This one I saw movement."

Standing, Max said, "Then we know what to do."

"Get down," Osorio said.

"No need. The kinds of things the Brotherhood is involved in — they don't do any of that until nighttime. They like the dark. If they left anybody inside to guard that warehouse, well, we've got a seasoned detective like you to protect us."

Drummond turned toward the warehouse. "I'll go check it out. Let you know if there's any trouble waiting for you."

But before the ghost could leave, Osorio looked from Max to Sandra with desperation wetting his eyes. "I've been suspended."

Drummond whirled back. "I knew it. I knew something was off about the way he approached this whole case. I told you this was all off the books."

Sandra rolled her eyes at Drummond before saying to Osorio, "It's okay. We don't need you to be an official police officer today."

Osorio reached down the neck of his shirt and produced a gold chain with a crucifix pendant. He closed his eyes and whispered words of prayer. Then he kissed the crucifix and stuck it back under his shirt. "When I confronted Cecily Hull at that fundraising event, I thought she was part of some Satanist group. You know the type? These people who go off in the woods, kill a couple cats or dogs or whatever, and screw around, pretending to cast magic spells. They can cause problems in a neighborhood, and for people as powerful as the Hulls, they can cause problems for an entire city. Rich people like that, they often take things too far. I didn't want to see her escalating from ringing the necks of a few chickens to kidnapping sweet girls like Ashley Cortez. You understand?"

"You were testing her," Max said.

"Yeah, that's a good word for it. I wanted to see her reaction, see how close I was to hitting the mark. I knew it was risky for my career, but I figured I might never have that opportunity again. So, I took it."

Drummond said, "I doubt he got what he was looking for. Probably something much worse."

"She didn't give me the reaction I expected. In fact, seeing the look in her eyes, the cold smirk on her lips — I'm telling you, right at that moment I started thinking that maybe there was something else to what I had been hearing about her. Not that magic is real, but that there are real activities being done by those who believe in it. What I thought were just people who had gotten together to find an excuse for bad and reckless behavior in her eyes, I saw a true belief that she could cast spells. That to her, magic was real."

"That's why you saw her again. Asked about the other cases."

Osorio didn't bother with a denial. "I thought she might let something slip."

Max's tumbling gut flipped again. "She gave you Brenda Byrd, didn't she?"

"Yeah."

"That's why you don't want to go in the warehouse. Afraid of the answer you might find."

"I'm not afraid to go in there. It's my job to go in. Just wanted you to understand that I still don't know if you're frauds or not, but I believe that you believe in what you're doing. If you are frauds, it's not on purpose. You're not a couple grifters trying to take advantage of people."

"What a relief. I'll be sure to tell my mom and all my friends."

"Don't be a jerk."

"It's better than sucker punching somebody."

Osorio looked down. "Oh, yeah. That. Sorry." He looked back at Max. "I truly am."

"You want to apologize? Have our backs as we go in that warehouse. Can you do that?"

Osorio stood and pulled a .38 from his shoulder holster. "I can."

With a clap of his hands, Drummond said, "Looks like I'm back on scout patrol. I'll let you know what I find."

Unable to explain to Osorio why they should suddenly wait

again, Max decided the best course would be to lead the way. Sandra came up by his side, and he could hear Osorio only a few steps behind. Max slowed his pace to give Drummond extra time. He figured it might also give Osorio a little confidence — seeing that the Porters didn't run blindly into the dangerous warehouse but approached with caution.

They reached a wood door that had once been painted white. Now, it had a gray, mottled tinge from mold. The frame split all around and a row of ants marched along the right side. Max glanced back to see that Osorio stood with his weapon at the ready. The detective gave Max a nod to say he had the door covered and it was safe to open. Well, *safe* was a relative word.

Max turned the dented knob and pushed the door in. He expected a wave of stale air and a heavy volume of dust. He got neither. No dust — somebody had been here recently enough to freshen up the entrance. No stale air — but a smell nonetheless. A bad smell. One that told Max plenty without Drummond's report.

The distinct smell of death.

# Chapter 17

A DILAPIDATED RECEPTION ROOM greeted them and a long hallway stretched down with doors along one side. Offices, Max guessed. At the end, double doors stood open and sharp beams of sunlight revealed the warehouse. Startled rats squeaked but managed to remain unseen.

From his pocket, Max dug out the mask he wore for crowds. It didn't help much, but it knocked back the smell a little. Sandra and Osorio did the same.

Passing through an office door, Drummond appeared in the corridor leading to the warehouse. "Not sure you really want to go in there, but I'm afraid you'll have to."

"He's here, isn't he?" Sandra said. "Samson Price. I can feel that same energy from the séance."

"Séance?" Osorio said.

Max pushed onward. "Everybody be quiet and stay focused."

"Who's Samson Price?"

"Not now."

Like a man surrendering to inevitable defeat, Drummond said, "You better make sure Detective Osorio holsters that weapon. Don't let them go in there until he does. Ashley Cortez didn't make it. And it gets worse. A lot worse."

"Damn." Max's mouth dropped as he struggled to find the right words to use with Osorio.

Sandra saved him when she turned back to the detective and said, "I think we can safely assume there's nobody here. If there had been, we would know it by now. Please, put the gun away."

While there were plenty of sensible arguments against doing so, Osorio's fear blinded him to such a debate. Sandra's clear tone led him along. With a shaking nod, he holstered the .38.

Max forged ahead toward the double doors. The stench grew stronger as they walked. With Ashley Cortez dead, Max guessed he would have limited time to get through to the detective. Once that man saw the girl's lifeless body, he would be running like a madman bent on revenge. Brenda would be in danger.

Before Max could place a plan in his head, though, they reached the end of the corridor and entered the warehouse. Cavernous, it still held towers of old crates, some reaching near the enormous ceiling. Bare bulbs hung on long wires spaced apart several feet. But instead of creating a hedge maze of wooden boxes, somebody had cleared away a large section in the middle.

Not somebody. The Brotherhood.

Drummond had softened the blow, but he undersold how bad the sight would be. Max's muscles clenched and Sandra covered her mouth as she gasped. Osorio fell to his knees. He crossed himself and bowed in prayer, the mumbled words shivering with tears.

On the floor, a casting triangle had been painted in thick, gobs of dark blood. Circles had been drawn around each point and a fourth circle had been formed within the triangle — out of salt. Along the outside edges of the triangle, strange symbols had been written. Some Max recognized from other spells he had witnessed, but most of the symbols reminded him of the ancient occult writing he had seen the Brotherhood use before.

On a table situated about ten feet to the left, Ashley Cortez's body had been stripped. As if undergoing an operation. No, an autopsy. Indeed, somebody had been practicing — a barbarian. Her chest had been shredded open and her organs ripped out. The heart had been set in one circle, her lungs in another, and her stomach in the third. All three had become wet lumps of meat, butchered by an unskilled hand. As horrid as all of it appeared, nothing turned Max's stomach like the sight of Ashley's legs. The skin bore the jagged marks of feasting rats.

Osorio pressed his head to the floor, his back rising and falling with each heavy shudder.

Within the salt circle, swirls of green mist spun under a gentle current. Leaning back toward Sandra, and keeping the gorge in his throat down, Max managed, "Is that Price?"

She nodded, her eyes locked on Ashley's abused corpse.

Drummond said, "You need to grab Osorio's .38 while he's still in shock. I expected him to take this bad, but he's looking a lot worse, very unstable."

Max had to agree. But he didn't like the idea of trying to relieve a seasoned detective of his firearm. At least it gave him an excuse to turn away from the harsh sight the Brotherhood had left.

Covering his face with both hands, Osorio arched back as if struck hard in the head. He howled. "Ashley!"

Max stepped over to the grieving policeman. He glanced back at his partner and his wife. They both made pushing motions, urging him to get on with it. Easy for them.

Reaching down with one hand toward the weapon and another hand to block any resistance, Max edged closer and closer. As if trying to nab a dangerous snake by the back of the head, he adjusted and readjusted, never quite getting close enough, knowing that at some point, he simply needed to act. But then Osorio dropped his hands and opened his eyes wide.

He stared at Max. Max stared back. Both frozen — one in confusion; the other in guilt.

"Oh crap," Drummond said.

With rapid motions, Osorio popped upward, seizing Max and pivoting him in a takedown. It was a modified wrestling move — something Max could recognize but had no muscle memory to successfully combat. In seconds, he lay on his back and Osorio straddled his waist.

"What are you trying to pull?" Osorio asked, his fist back and ready. "Did you have something to do with this? Is that why the two of you are here? Did you do that to Ashley?"

Max pressed against Osorio's chest but could not budge the man. "No, no. You've got it wrong."

"Why'd you do this? Huh? You working for this Samson Price?"

"It's like we told you — we found out about this place when

we were searching for —"

"A séance, right? That's what you said. A freaking séance."

Sandra stepped into view, utilizing her soft voice once again. "I understand how upset you are. But I think —"

"You don't understand a damn thing. Both of you aren't telling me the truth. Not the real thing. Not the full truth. But you're going to start right now. Even if I have to beat your husband to a pulp in order to get it."

From his position, Max could only see Sandra upside down. But he also saw a pale figure pass behind her and come around. Drummond. The ghost took up a position to the side of Osorio.

"Give the word, and I've got him," he said.

Sandra raised her hands up to her shoulders and out. "We're not trying anything. This is not a trap. Everything we told you is true. Brenda had nothing to do with this, we do know about the Brotherhood, and they are the ones responsible for what happened to Ashley."

Tears streamed down Osorio's face. "That poor girl."

"It's not fair. Nobody deserves that."

"You all know what this is about. And you're going to tell me." He wrapped Max's shirt in his fist and yanked. Max winced, bracing for the hit.

"If that's what you want," Sandra said. "You want the full truth, then you got it. You're about to feel very cold. That's the touch of a ghost."

"Ghosts? Don't lie to me about —"

Drummond sliced his hand across Osorio's back. The man dropped Max, bolted to his feet, and staggered backwards. "What the hell?"

Getting up, brushing off the warehouse dirt, Max said, "I'd tell you that's our other partner — the ghost of a detective — but you wouldn't believe me."

"Aw, get out of my face. That sweet girl is dead over there and you're telling me this bull. What kind of sick-minded fool are you?"

"Drummond, again please."

This time Osorio screeched when he felt the chill of the

ghost. "It's a trick, right?"

"It doesn't really matter. A few hours from now, you'll come up with some reason in your head to deny any of it happening. Unless …"

"What?"

"You accept what you know is true. You believe us."

Despite the terrified confusion wrinkling Osorio's face, he managed to say, "Ghosts are real?" He looked around the warehouse, his eyes slowing across the spell of the floor and Ashley's slaughtered body. "And this? Is there really something to this?" His shoulders slouched. "Oh, Lord." With a sigh, he looked from Max to Sandra. Then, moving slow and careful, he removed his .38 and handed it to Sandra.

"Thank you," she said.

Osorio lowered his head, and in silence, his shoulders shook. He pressed his fingers against his eyes, sniffed hard, and let out a short gasp. Then, with a sharp inhale: "Don't worry. You have nothing to fear from me. I don't know what to make of all this, but that girl deserves justice. This Brotherhood and whatever they did on the floor and however you chilled my skin — ghosts or some trick — I'm starting to think that the only way I'm going to get that justice is by helping you."

"That may very well be true."

"But I'm warning you — if you're lying to me, I will find a way to put you both behind bars."

Max said, "Fair enough." He put out his hand and Osorio gave a cautious shake.

A noise from the corridor snapped everybody's attention, and before Drummond could float over to check it out, Brenda Byrd stepped into the warehouse. Sweat stained her blouse, and her eyes stared with cold vacancy. She moved in a shuffling motion, dragging one foot behind like a zombie in a B-grade horror flick.

Sandra stepped forward. "Now's another chance for you to do some believing."

"Why?" Osorio said. "You going to tell me she's a ghost?"

"No. But she's possessed by one. Samson Price."

He greened as he inched back from the group. Max grabbed

him by the arm, stopping Osorio from disrupting the casting triangle. "Watch where you're going."

Brenda halted. Drool fell from her mouth as she stared ahead. Circling her, Drummond looked from the woman to the swirls of green mist in the center of the spell.

Answering the question on Max's mind, Sandra said, "The séance must have created a stronger connection between the two. Samson had been trying to link with her all this time, and after we succeeded with the séance, that link is now healthy. Strong. For a little longer, anyway."

"Yeah," Drummond said, scratching his jaw. "Out with it, Samson. You've gone to this much trouble, and you see we've made it to the warehouse — what is it you want to say?"

The green mist brightened as Brenda's jaw moved up and down. "Diamond," she said, her voice channeling Mr. Price.

"Diamonds? Our crack researcher says you were a miner. Is that what you mined?"

"Jim," Brenda said.

"Who's Jim?" Osorio asked.

Nobody answered. Nobody knew.

"Hidden," Brenda said. "Lucas." She raised a hand and pointed at the Brotherhood's spell. "Help." She collapsed.

With a burst of speed, Osorio leapt across the room, sweeping Brenda up into his arms as he growled the word *No.* He checked her pulse and held her close. "No, no. Not one more death today."

"You can relax," Sandra said. "She's not dying. Just possessed, that's all. Probably will wake up with a bad headache."

His brief bout of anger at Death and the cruelty of existence withered down to the confusion of a child attempting to comprehend a foreign language. "Possessed? Like in *The Exorcist?*"

"That's demonic possession. Different thing. This was simply a ghost trying to use her in order to communicate with us. Not harm her." She pointed to the green mist. "That ghost over there."

Max inclined his head toward the spell. "Do you think you

can break that? Free him?"

Standing with her arms crossed and her head cocked, she turned an intense focus toward the horrible lines painted upon the floor. Studying the spell, she held still as if carved from marble. The longer she stayed in that position, the more worried Max became — he had expected an answer quickly. She knew the limits of her abilities quite well.

"What is the matter with you people?" Osorio's words built in strength but could not hide the trembling desperation skirting underneath. "How can you be so casual? You talk about having a ghost for a partner and demonic possession and green mists and all of this, but — but it can't be real. That's the answer, isn't it? The only reason you people are fine with this stuff is because you know it's not real. You know what's actually going on."

Without taking his eyes off his wife, Max said, "Tell yourself whatever you need. Just don't get in our way."

Clicking his tongue, Drummond floated over to join Max. "I really thought we had a moment there where he might accept things. He's still teetering on the edge, but it's going to take another shocker to get him to believe the truth."

Max said, "I'm not really giving him any more thought. If he can help us, great, but we've got big problems to deal with. This spell was put here by the Brotherhood. We only dealt with them once before, and I sort of hoped that was it."

"Yeah, but you knew it wouldn't be."

"I said it was a hope."

"Partner, sometimes you can play the odds, but you have to know what those odds are. Any reasonable assessment of the Brotherhood should've told you it was one in a hundred against that they would take their defeat and walk away. Not the kind of thing you want to gamble on."

Sandra shifted her weight to one leg which Max took as a sign that he could speak to her. "Hon," he said. "You got anything?"

"A lot of questions," she said. "The construction is basic, and obviously there's blood magic being used, but all the writing around the edges — that's the strange part. Usually, the writing is within the casting circle or, in this case, the triangle. That's important. All the energy a witch uses to focus a spell has to exist within the boundary of the shape drawn."

"Okay. That is different. But the writing is what the Brotherhood used before."

"And that took me a long time to crack."

"Does that mean we can't break the lines and destroy the curse? That usually works."

Sandra raised an eye. "Do you remember what happened the very first time you broke a spell that way?"

A fire. He would never forget. He had been strapped to a chair, about to be cursed much like Drummond had been in the 1940s. But Max broke the circle, and when the spell went off, he was blasted across the room. A fire broke out. Nearly killed him and Sandra.

"Point made," he said. "Aside from pulling Samson Price out of whatever lies beyond and returning him here, do you know what the purpose of this is?"

"I couldn't guess. Not yet. But before we mess with this spell, we need to find that out."

From behind, Osorio said, "She's waking up. Hey, hey. She's waking up."

They turned to find Brenda sitting cross-legged, dazed and clutching her head. Osorio crouched next to her, rubbing her back and whispering softly.

"Brenda?" Sandra said easing down next to her. "What do you remember?"

Raising her head, Brenda stared across the warehouse floor, settling on the green mist trapped in the center of the spell. Her eyes glistened as she opened her mouth. She whipped her focus straight into Sandra. "This is the place. The big empty place in my dreams."

"We know."

"Samson. You have to help Samson. He's in such pain. Whatever they did to bring him back, they did it wrong. Or maybe it's because they should never have done it in the first place. I thought this was about me, but it's not. He needs my help — our help." Scrunching her face, she looked at Osorio.

"Who are you?"

With a calming voice, Max stepped forward. "That is Detective Jorge Osorio, and he's going to guard you for a while. Jorge, we need you to do what you've been trained for. Take her home, keep her safe, be a good police officer. Don't worry about the rest."

Osorio nodded at first, but then his face froze as he stared at the blood dripping off Ashley's body on the table. "I have to call that in."

Drummond said, "I can freeze him."

Max put out his hand. "Don't do that."

Assuming the command was directed at him, Osorio scowled. "I have to. I can't let that go. It's my duty."

"How are you going to explain any of this? Right now, we can't break that spell without harming the soul trapped in the center. If you call in Ashley's murder, this warehouse will be swarming with cops. They don't know what they're doing. Not with this. They'll take pictures of the spell — which might be dangerous in itself — and when they're done processing the scene, they'll send in a cleanup crew. If they haven't destroyed the spell by that point, the cleanup crew will, and Samson Price's spirit will be ripped to pieces again. You want to be responsible for what is essentially a murder?"

"No, but —"

Sandra said, "Please, let us do our job. When we're finished, once we've found a way to save Samson Price, then we'll let you know."

Osorio's frightened gaze crossed the room, unable to find safety, and returned to Sandra. "You want to save Samson Price?"

"Yes."

"And he's a ghost?"

"That's right. When we're done, when it's safe to call this into the police, you can do so. If that's what you want."

"Why wouldn't I?"

"It's been our experience that the police are not always understanding about magic. I think that's been your experience, too. To them, it's a threat to keeping the peace. Most people in authority think that if the paranormal could ever be proven, there would be chaos running in the streets."

"And since you already got yourself mixed up with Cecily Hull on that front," Max said, "you may not want to be associating yourself with all of this. At least, not in the eyes of your bosses."

Osorio clamped his mouth tight as he looked over the horrible warehouse bloodbath. He stood and straightened his shirt. With one hand pressed against his chest — possibly pushing his crucifix harder against his skin — he offered his other hand to Brenda. "You're safe now. I'm a detective with the police department. Going to take you home and watch over you." To Max and Sandra, he added, "I'm not sure what I'm going to do, but it can't wait long. We found Ashley; somebody else will, too. And her family needs to know. They shouldn't have to suffer more. So, you do what you need to do, and then call me. I'll figure it out from there."

"Thank you," Max said. He turned to Drummond. "I need you to try talking with Samson here. If that doesn't work, maybe part of him is in the Other and you can talk with him there."

"I doubt it. Doesn't usually work that way." Drummond drifted over toward the edge of the spell. "But I'll see what I can do."

"Sandra's going to research the spell and I'll do what I can to figure out who Jim is. Or was. Or Lucas. As much pain as Samson Price is in at the moment, I can't believe he said those names for nothing."

With a firm clap of his hands, Drummond said, "Then let's get to it."

# Chapter 18

WHILE PART OF MAX HATED leaving Samson Price's tortured spirit stuck in that spell and Ashley Cortez's desecrated body lying on that table, part of him lightened as he added distance from that warehouse. Focusing on the afternoon traffic gave his mind something normal to lock upon, something every day, something to help push away the agonizing sights he had witnessed. But burying those images would only get him through the moment. If his mind could not find some sane release, these horrors would seep into his dreams. He had never considered therapy before — never seriously — but with each successive case they undertook, with the growing number of sights he had to bury in order to function, the more he thought he better start talking to somebody. Either that or suffer a PTSD breakdown.

He glanced over at Sandra. She had spent her whole life seeing ghosts. All ghosts. For her, the trauma was not in the supernatural but rather the sadistic nature of everyday people. Ashley Cortez's corpse disturbed her far more than a ghost. It could be the worst horror they had experienced yet.

He hated that he had to use the word *yet.*

Sandra pointed to the sign for Route 52. "Get on the highway and head south."

"We're not going home?"

"You have your laptop with you?"

"Of course."

"Then you can do research anywhere. But for me — I don't have the resources at home, and they're not online. Not for this kind of spell. This is going to take some seriously old and rare books."

As Max sped along the on-ramp to 52 South, goosebumps

ran along his arms. "Does that mean we're going to a witch's house?"

"More like a private library for witches. But it's not called a library. Also, it's in Lexington. If we run late, you'll have an excuse to get barbecue for dinner."

Max grinned. He couldn't help it. Being known so well spread warmth through his chest. That didn't last long, however, because he noticed Sandra's bouncing knee. "Something you're not telling me about this library?"

Sandra forced her knee to stop. "It's not a library."

"Don't evade the question. What's wrong with this place?"

"It's not that. It's Ashley Cortez's body."

"Yeah. I was thinking about that, too. Perhaps we should both consider seeing a psychologist. Somebody to help us with all the stuff we've gone through."

Sandra turned her head. "You are full of surprises. It's not a bad thought, and we should talk about that later, but that's not what I was thinking. The thing is that having her body cut open like that, having her organs already placed in circles, suggests the spell is much further along than I'm comfortable with. I'm not sure how tight a timeline we're on — hopefully, that's part of what I'll learn — but I know we can't do this at our leisure."

Without thinking about it, Max's foot pressed harder on the accelerator.

Max had questions. A few. Somewhere between twelve and twelve hundred. However, he recognized that most of the answers would come when they arrived at this strange building. He only had to be patient.

The journey south did little to ease his mind. They exited the highway near Lexington Hospital, and the road stretched all the way to the center of town. They never went that far, though. Taking side streets and back roads, they weaved their way further southward, avoiding all the major commercial roads, cruising through one suburban neighborhood after another. Soon, the houses thinned out, becoming smaller with larger acreage. Thick woods filled the land between. On Old Linwood Road, they sped by house after house until Sandra motioned for Max to slow down. Route 85 crossed nearby, just out of sight, and when she pointed to the house on the right, Max wondered if there was a convenient on-ramp — in case they had to make a fast exit.

The house stood back from the road — a one-story rancher painted blue with a gravel driveway and a well-maintained yard. A sign boasting a security service gave the home a normal, average look. To the layperson, not the kind of place that would be lodging a coven of witch librarians.

Sandra pointed to a dirt road barely visible in the back. "The house is where they live. But we're going further that way. They call it Haven House."

"The house or the library?"

"The house doesn't have a name. And don't call it a library. They don't like that."

Barely wide enough for one car, the dirt road meandered through the woods like a lazy snake. Max had to hope nobody came the other way. If he had his bearings correct, and he usually did, the Lexington Airport had been carved out of these woods on the opposite side. It was a small municipal airport, but it also represented another form of escape should they need it.

Whether a trick of the light or his rising nerves, the pines and oaks appeared to close in, darkening around them. Then again, just because Max continued to use the word *library* to describe the place did not mean it would be welcoming to him. After all, the word *witch* had been used in conjunction. Naming it Haven House did even less to lend assurance.

The road curved left and opened into a small, gravel parking area. An old blue pickup occupied one of the spaces. Max performed a multipoint turn so that he faced the dirt road out — should it be necessary. If Sandra found his precautions silly or amusing, she said nothing. In fact, he thought she flashed a look of satisfaction.

"Have you ever been here before?" he asked.

"Of course. How else would I have known it was here? You sound surprised that witches are organized enough to have this place. But you've seen they have covens and retirement facilities."

"I guess. You sure about these witches? That they're safe?"

"As safe as any witch."

"That's not very reassuring."

With a sly wink, she said, "Bring your work, sit down at a table, and ignore everything else. Don't talk with them. Don't get curious about what they're doing. Keep out of everything."

"You're not inspiring confidence."

"You'll be fine. It's not like you haven't dealt with witches before."

Getting out of the car, he said, "Exactly. I know how dangerous they can be."

She led the way up the stone path. "Relax. These are librarian witches."

"Except it's not a library, right?"

"Think of it more like a book repository. The ladies here can be a bit fickle about lending the books out."

"Yeah, well, I'd hate to see how they handle an overdue book."

Less than a minute later, they stood before a stone house. It had to have been a couple hundred years old yet remained in impeccable condition. Modern touches, including solar panels on the roof and a keypad lock, did not take away from the authentic feel of stepping back into history. From what Max could see, the building maintained a large rectangular shape — *large* being the operative word. With two visible stories — and Max had no doubt there would be several more beneath the ground as well — he guessed the original occupants had farmed the land and raised a large family. They needed the space to house everybody. Ten people could easily fit and have room for many more.

A polished wood porch lined the front. As Sandra stepped up toward the main door — a dark wood finished with stained glass inlays — she moved with familiarity and confidence. Max marveled. Even if she felt half the nerves he felt, she knew how to comport herself in the presence of witches.

"In case you had other plans in mind," she said, "let me do the talking. In fact, though I know it will be difficult, do your best not to say anything at all."

From her purse, she pulled out her wallet. From her wallet, she pulled out a small card. And reading from that card, she punched in a number on the keypad. The front door lock clicked open, and they entered the witch building lost in the middle of the woods.

*Wonderful.*

# Chapter 19

NO MATTER HOW MANY TIMES Max had entered the homes and businesses belonging to witches, he never grew entirely comfortable with it. Probably a good thing. Often, they were cramped spaced, overflowing with clutter piled high and foreboding thickening air. The smell of all the desperate souls who had crossed those thresholds to deal with a witch permeated the walls of whatever dwelling they encountered. This library felt no different.

Except, no matter what they called it, this place was a library. Hallowed ground as far as Max was concerned. And anybody who seriously accepted the title of *Librarian* had to agree with the sentiment. Max could not conceive of a person wanting to be a librarian and not feeling such reverence for books and knowledge.

Finding common ground with witches soured his stomach.

The interior appeared much as Max guessed it had always looked. Numerous doors and halls that opened into living rooms, bedrooms, storage spaces, a kitchen, a playroom, and more. But while the layout remained untouched for centuries, their use had been repurposed. The wide foyer which included a narrow staircase leading up to the second floor now had a desk with a high counter. Glancing in any direction revealed bookshelves upon bookshelves — each stuffed with dusty volumes, old binders, and yellowed papers.

Behind the desk, a woman stood. She had wrinkled, dark skin and snowy hair, a slight stoop and cracking lips, and thick glasses with a beaded chain latching them around her neck. She bore the quiet authority required to maintain order in such a place while also appearing kind enough that one could ask a question and feel comfortable that she would have the answer. To Max, she looked every bit the witch and every bit the librarian.

"Good morning," she said. "Welcome to Haven House."

Max peeked at his phone — almost noon, still technically morning. It had been a long one, indeed.

The witch squinted, pressed her glasses tighter against her face, and grinned a crooked smile. "Sandra Porter. So nice to see you again."

"It's good to see you, too." Sandra stepped to the side and gestured to Max. "Madame Novak, this is my husband."

"Ah, Max Porter. A pleasure to finally meet you." Madame Novak put out her hand.

He hesitated, but she did not appear to take offense. At Sandra's urging — mostly a sharp motion with her head — Max gave the witch a gentle handshake. He wanted to drop a quick bit of sarcastic commentary, mostly out of habit — he found it often helped even the dynamics with witches if they thought he was calm enough to issue wisecracks — but he heeded Sandra's words in the car. A simple nod, and he gave his attention to his wife. The witch did, too.

"How have you and your sisters been?" Sandra asked.

Madame Novak's mouth turned down in a caricature of sadness. "I'm afraid we had a break-in a few weeks ago."

Max coughed. "Who would be crazy enough to steal from witches?"

"I suppose the ignorant or those who wish to die." She spoke so plainly, it shriveled Max's gut worse than any sinister tone. She went on, "But our problems will get solved. No worries. Let's solve your problems. What can I help you with today?"

As she and Sandra conversed in hushed tones appropriate for a library, Max noticed two framed photographs next to the entrance. They were black and white photos. The first depicted seven women standing in a line. Based on the clothing, Max pegged the time period around the 1950s. On the right side of the line, Madame Novak stood, not quite as old as now but not young enough to be in a photo from seventy years ago. The second framed photograph must have been from the late-1970s and showed Madame Novak along with two other women — both from the previous picture as well. In another life, this would have frightened him. But in Max's peculiar world, he had come into contact with several witches that had extended their lives beyond normal.

"That's Madame Fein and Madame Weir." The boney finger pointing at the women appeared on Max's right and he fought down the urge to yelp. Madame Novak smelled of old newspaper, and when she turned back to Sandra, she brushed Max's elbow — a shocking jolt ran up his arm. "We three are all that's left of the original coven. The newcomers are every bit as much sister to us, though. Still, it's hard to let go of the ones we love." To Sandra, she said, "Come, come, now child. Let's see if we can find some answers for you."

As the old woman headed through a door on the left, Sandra said, "Is there a place that Max can do some work while he waits?"

"Of course. Lots of places. Pick wherever calls out."

Half-joking, Max said, "Do I need a wi-fi password?"

"It's *eye of newt* — no spaces, all lowercase."

As Sandra left, the old witch leaning on her arm with the touch of a loving grandmother, Max didn't know whether to be amused or terrified. He chose neither. His muscles ached to run after Sandra and rip her away from the witch. He held back. Instead, he turned his mind toward the search for a worktable.

Room after room opened Max to a bevy of surprising treasures. In this converted house hidden deep in a forest, he found a cherrywood shelf with carved ivory figures on the corners, a bearskin rug with the head still attached, and a marble fireplace with an original Renoir hanging above the mantelpiece. He spotted a shelf of fiction with books that appeared to be all first editions — Kipling, Kafka, Tolstoy, Dickens, Poe, Hemingway, and Steinbeck. In a small room that had once been used for sewing, Max discovered a collection of LPs spanning genres from classical to hard rock, from country to punk, from disco to EDM. Every record he inched outward had been signed. In many cases — such as the Beatles, Led Zeppelin, Van Halen, and Pearl Jam — signed by the entire band.

Walking by a door with the word OFFICE painted in neat script, he noticed a long, thin room that may have been where the original occupants kept their finer dishes and silverware — though Max found it hard to believe they had reason to own such things in the middle of nowhere. Yet one side of the closet-like room had a hutch from floor to ceiling. Where dishes would have been displayed behind glass, old texts now sat. Texts with titles like *First Spells for the Art of Witchcraft, Purity and Pestilence,* and *The Barrow Coven (1212-1347).* On the far end, near a window looking out on the gravel parking lot, he found a book with the simple, haunting title *Madness.*

The book had been propped on a stand, its cover faced out at an angle, revealing a dark leather front with gold lettering and several lines pressed in. It took Max a few moments to decipher the lines into a recognizable picture — almost like staring at those computer-drawn abstracts that would eventually reveal a 3D image.

A face. That's what Max saw. A distraught woman, her deep-set eyes staring back at him with misgivings and deceit, her hair hanging unkempt. She bore an animalistic threat.

He found it strange how a mere grouping of lines — slashes and swirls — could form such a detailed image. One that seemed to look back at him, to have a consciousness, to sit on the verge of reaching through its leather background and offering a hand. The threat, he saw now, had not been one of danger but rather adventure. A promise of thrilling days and insatiable nights.

The world disappeared into a mist that only allowed him to see the book. With a greedy hand, he reached out for it. But a feather voice said, "Oh, dear, that's enough of that."

At first, Max thought the book had spoken to him. He narrowed his eyes upon it, waiting for a command or a lure — or an offer. But then a wrinkled hand gently pushed his outstretched fingers aside. The fog encircling him snapped away. Not even a puff. Just gone. He stood in that small room in the witch library, and the wide face of a grandmother looked up at him.

Her kind eyes promised fresh baked cookies while her gentle smile cleared away all darkness. The intoxication that had whirled around him sobered in her presence.

He blushed. "I shouldn't have touched that."

"You didn't."

"I didn't?"

"No, bless your heart."

"Still, I'm sorry."

"Ho ho, not half as sorry as you would've been if Madame Fein had not shown up."

"I take it you're Madame Fein?"

"Who else?" She could not have been five feet tall — and that was a stretch — and her face could not have been flatter. Her nose barely bumped from the surface of her skin. When she closed her mouth, her lips disappeared entirely. She moved with little shuffling steps as if anything faster might dislodge the mass of gray, unkempt hair sitting atop her head. To Max, she looked more librarian than witch — though he did not fool himself into thinking she had no witch in her — and he decided right then that he kind of liked Madame Fein.

Toddling towards the door, she waved him to follow. "Come along now. Madame Fein knows a place that you can sit and work without getting into any trouble."

Max wanted to ask her about the book, about what kind of spell enchanted or cursed it. He wanted to know what system they used to categorize all these odd books. He wondered if they had histories of covens as well. Probably, he figured. But with so many rooms, yet still limited space, how did they decide what was worth keeping and what they could afford to discard? As these queries flooding his mind grew deeper, he remembered Sandra's cautions. He would follow Madame Fein to another room but not engage in conversation.

Despite his head still being a fuzz of cotton, he managed to stay with Madame Fein through the maze of the corridors and book stacks. Understanding where she took him and how to get out was another matter — one he failed. But after two hallways, several rooms of varying sizes, and a downward incline, Madame

Fein finally indicated an archway on her left.

Awash in books, the room lacked windows — or perhaps the numerous towers of texts occluded all sunlight. In two corners, high-backed chairs had been placed with gooseneck reading lamps cutting a swath out of the dark. Light-purple and stuffed with comfort, the chairs invited the reader to curl up and lounge through whatever volume had pulled their interest. In the center, seemingly supported by more books, a wood table with mosaic inlays in the middle waited for Max.

"This should do for you." Madame Fein brushed off unseen dirt from the table. She gathered a few books from one end and carelessly stacked them on the nearest pile. "Now, you do your best to stay in this room. None of the books here will bother you. Should you need anything, anything at all, you simply have to push that button." She indicated an old doorbell installed next to the archway. "Madame Fein will take care of you."

Setting his laptop on the table, Max said, "I'm sure this will be perfect."

"Naturally."

As she left the room, he shivered. Whatever that book had done to him had cleared. He felt normal again. But he believed Madame Fein may have saved his sanity. He also discovered that he had no worries for Sandra. She had used this place before, and it made no sense for the witch librarians to harm other witches. Not here. Though Sandra's status as a witch may not have satisfied all of her sisterhood, he did not see how hurting their clientele helped their business. He would simply have to wait for Sandra to retrieve him. Until then, he had the research.

Unfortunately, he had little more to go on.

# Chapter 20

TWO NAMES. TWO WORDS. *Lucas, Jim, hidden, diamond.* He wrote them down and stared at them. Anagrams? Possibly. But it had been Max's experience that while such machinations might be used by witches to hide the true meanings within their books — though they preferred codes and dead languages — rarely would someone be cryptic when trying to be clear. With only the energy to convey four words, Price had chosen these four. *Lucas, Jim, hidden, diamond.* That had to be enough.

*Maybe it is.* Max looked at the words closer because he recognized that he knew a little more information which could help narrow a search into something useable. Namely, these words had to be linked to North Carolina and to Samson Price. Knowing that also suggested these links would occur during Price's lifetime which cut down the possible years to search as well.

"Not so bad, after all," he said to the empty room as he woke up his laptop and connected to the internet.

But even with those parameters, the keywords he had available were generic to the point of being practically useless. Even the names Lucas and Jim were so common that they could be referring to anybody.

*Unless they're Price's children.*

Max pulled up the census reports he had used to find the Samson Price-Brenda Byrd connection. According to those records, however, none of his progeny bore either name he searched for.

That left the words *hidden* and *diamond.* But *hidden diamond* seemed as fruitless as it was far-fetched. Max did it anyway, and the results were as numerous (over twenty million hits) as they were impractical (loads of puzzle games and conspiracy sites).

He leaned back and pursed his lips. There had to be some angle that would work. After all, a soul as desperate as Samson Price would not waste his efforts with meaningless or valueless words.

"It's not right," a grinding voice said as heavy steps clumped down the hall. A moment later, a woman crossed right by Max's view. A witch — presumably Madame Weir. Tall, skeletal, her bony fingers pilled her black skirt as she walked. Her stern mouth — a thin line of cracked stitches which might have been wrinkles once — opened and closed as she mumbled. Max thought she spoke to herself, but then a darker thought hit him — perhaps she intended for him to hear every word.

"He's spoiling our books." She moved with all the vigor of a toy on dying batteries. Perhaps she could move faster and chose a deliberate pace so Max would have to endure more of her verbal assaults. "He talks nonsense. All those words he uses adding up to a mound of nothingness."

Right when Max thought she would disappear down the hall, she stopped. She turned her gaunt face in his direction. One pale-gray eye glowered at him. The other remain closed, the muscles twitching at the corner.

A sickened, burning sensation formed in the center of Max's chest. Bile raced up his throat. When he swallowed it back, he winced at the sour burn.

And she was gone. He heard the clumps recede, and the mumbling continued.

Max sat still. He stared at the empty archway. He wanted to return to his work, but forgetting the frightening glare of a witch was never easy. It hovered before him like an omen, a dark specter promising to disrupt his peace. The way she spoke of him, showing disgust at not just a word or two, but everything he said. She lumped his words into a ball and spit them out. She took the most innocent phrases, the most useless utterances and—

Thoughts pinged around his brain, and the thrill of possibly solving a research problem electrified his body. Such a simple idea, yet it took a witch's offhanded insult for Max to see. *A mound,* she had said. His words were a *mound.* Lumped all together.

Pulling up a search bar, he typed in all four words that Samson Price had said — *diamond, Lucas, hidden, Jim.* He also added *North Carolina* and the word *mining* for good measure. All lumped together in a mound. As if debating the launch of a nuclear arsenal, Max's finger hovered over the enter key, a small quake revealing the state of his nerves.

He pressed the button.

In an instant, the results arrived. While scrolling down revealed entries that shared one or two of the parameters (and some that had no business being on the results page at all), only the first link covered every single word. It screamed that it was the right one. Max's research instincts jangled as he stared at the screen — James Paul Lucas, a.k.a. Diamond Jim, who lived in a small North Carolina town called Hiddenite up through 1947. And as icing on the cake, Hiddenite boasted an active emerald mine.

"Found you."

"And I found you," Sandra said, leaning on the archway. She had one thick book and two slim volumes in her arms. "Ready for lunch?"

Max glanced at his search results again. He typed the town into his maps program and saw the saddest news of all. "I'm afraid Lexington barbecue is off for today."

"Why? What did you find?"

"The town of Hiddenite. It's over an hour away, and it's where Samson Price wants us to go."

# Chapter 21

WHEN THEY HIT THE ROAD, Sandra opened one of her books and started reading. Max let the numbness of highway driving take over. At least, he tried to. The steady drone of wheels on pavement only blurred into the background, leaving him in contemplative quiet. But he did not like the thoughts that entered his mind.

He couldn't banish the image of Ashley Cortez — soaked in blood, carved open with callous abandon. Her eyes wide in shock, her body prone in death. Her excavated torso a vile desecration that refused to be ignored. Max tried. But she kept coming back.

He turned on the radio, keeping the volume low, and found a crackling station playing an old Tom Petty tune about the difficulty of waiting. Sandra paused her work to look over at him.

"It's hard to focus with the music," she said gently.

"Oh." He turned the radio off.

He managed a full five minutes — an eternity — but then his hands drummed out a rhythm. The back of his mind knew it was an annoying thing to do, and he didn't get much pleasure out of the act, either. But even thinking about annoyance kept Ashley Cortez under the surface, kept her image away from his consciousness.

"Honey, please. These are difficult texts to read and understand."

"Sorry," he said, stretching his fingers outward before regripping the steering wheel. He succeeded at another ten minutes of silence before an involuntary sigh rolled out from his chest.

Closing her book, Sandra said, "What's bothering you?"

He opened his mouth but did not know what to answer. If he brought up Ashley Cortez, that would bring the girl's image to his mind. He considered admitting that he had nearly touched one of the books at the witch library. But then he would have to describe what he experienced, and he had yet to understand it himself. Besides, Sandra had enough to be concerned with. He even had the notion that he should tell her about Drummond — about what he saw happen to Drummond during the séance. But that was not for him to tell. Heck, it had not been for him to see in the first place.

"I don't know," he finally said. As the words left him, he realized they were true. All those things bothered him, but he could not say which one sat at the core of his stress.

"Is it your mother?" she asked.

Max pulled off Route 40 and onto a long stretch of 64 West bracketed by hills, thick trees, and the occasional crossroad. Based on the road names — Smith Farm Road and Lackey Farm Road — there had to be farms nearby, tucked out of sight. "We'll be there soon."

While he kept his eyes forward, he could feel Sandra staring at him. She said, "Are you really not going to talk?"

"I don't know what to say. It's not my mother. But it's not *not* my mother, too. Maybe it's everything."

"What kind of everything?"

Before blurting out the name Ashley, Drummond, or saying anything he would later regret, Max took a deep breath and readjusted the rearview mirror. At length, he said, "One of the things I've been thinking about, about my mother, is how the Brotherhood has pulled back Samson Price's soul. The man had died, he had moved on, he went to whatever lies beyond, and he clearly did not want to return. Now I've learned to accept that the work we do puts you in danger, puts me in danger, the boys and even Drummond. Sometimes, it could even put my mother in danger. Those risks are things we've learned to live with. But the idea that someday after my mother has died and moved on, that a witch or the Brotherhood or a coven could one day rip her out of a much better existence, tear her back to this world against her will — it's too much. It's not right. But I don't see how we can do anything about it. That goes double for your soul or the boys."

"Honey, you don't need to worry. There's a reason we've never seen this before. The kind of magic that the Brotherhood has been attempting — big surprise — is rare and extremely difficult. Witchcraft is supposed to harness the natural energies of the world surrounding us and redirect them with purpose. But the Brotherhood — trying to summon inhuman spirits, trying to recall human souls, trying to rip apart a soul — these are unnatural acts. Things nature does not want to do even if it could. Witches, in general, don't mess with this kind of magic."

"What about Madame Ti?"

"Cecily Hull's little pet has tried but failed. In fact, if you want to be specific, we stopped her. We will stop the Brotherhood, too. You know it."

"It's not about if we'll stop them or not — and I hope it, not know it — but it's more about what they could do to the ones I love before I have a chance to stop them."

She reached out and took his hand. "You can't live other people's lives for them. Their happiness, their triumphs and miseries, everything they are and do is not your responsibility."

"I know that."

"I don't think so. If you did, we wouldn't be having this conversation."

Max let that cyclone around his stomach as Sandra returned to her work. She grumbled and flipped pages and made little twitches with her mouth. The charming cuteness of his wife — perhaps things only he found endearing — eased his troubled soul a fraction.

A short while later, Sandra closed her book, thought a moment, and pulled out her phone. "We need Brenda here."

"We do?"

"You said Samson Price wants us to go here. Everything I'm reading about these old spells says to me that if we're going to stop this, then we'll need something to connect with Price when the time comes. She's all we've got."

Max didn't like the idea of subjecting Brenda to anymore that day, but he trusted that Sandra wouldn't call on Brenda unless absolutely necessary. He also trusted that Brenda would be eager to keep participating. But there was another problem. "What about Osorio? He's watching her."

"I'm texting her to make an excuse or sneak out the bathroom window or something. He's not expecting her to be a flight risk."

"But once he knows she's gone —"

"He can search for her. But he doesn't know where we are. Heck, I don't know where we are."

"Open my laptop. The address should still be open. Have her meet us there. By the time we finish our lunch and go to where I want to take you, she'll be arriving."

After a few texts, Sandra pocketed her phone. "I really hope I'm wrong."

Max wanted to ask more, but they approached the town of Hiddenite. Several old factories and rundown businesses greeted them as they crossed the train tracks that bordered the town. Kudzu covered these buildings and the surrounding land like a disease. Just off to the right, Max saw The Yellow Deli — the restaurant Google promised to be the best local eatery around. There were only three to choose from.

As he headed toward the parking lot, he noticed how some of the streets looked like picturesque, smalltown Norman Rockwell paintings. Yet one block over, trailer homes that had not been cared for in decades prevailed. One block had gleaming new cars and manicured lawns. The other had rusting vehicles and dirt patches.

Stepping into The Yellow Deli, however, erased his sense of a poverty-stricken, backwoods populace. The multileveled restaurant had been built out of heavy woods, well-polished, with balconies overlooking the other floors straight down to the bottom. Tables had been set up along the balconies as well as in every private nook giving the place an open yet personal feel. The food smelled good, too.

A woman wearing a heavy, floor-length skirt as well as a plain blouse closed tight around the neck directed them up a spiraling staircase and along the second floor to their table. She had a bright, peaceful way about her, yet an odd twinkle in her eye.

A young man approached, welcomed them to the restaurant, asked if his wife had taken their drink order and then left to give them a few moments to look over the menu.

"Did he say his *wife?* I swear that's what I heard," Max said.

"Apparently the two are married. It's a small town. Besides, do you have a problem with spouses working together?"

Looking over the balcony gave Max a clear view of the kitchen, and he watched as two women prepared deli sandwiches — each dressed in the same floor-length skirts and overly conservative blouses. "They remind me of Mennonite women without the headpieces."

"It says in the menu that they all are part of a group church."

"Really?" He looked at the introduction written in the menu. "Says they all live on a plot of land just out of town. Like a commune."

"Or a cult."

"Like a witch cult?"

Sandra paused to observe the restaurant staff with serious consideration. After a moment, she said, "I don't think so. Just devout to their faith."

"Good. Because I'm hungry, and I wouldn't want to have to go searching for another place to eat."

After ordering and being served, Sandra said, "Since you're the hungry one, I'll go first. You eat, I'll talk."

Max had already bitten into his sandwich. Chewing, he nodded.

Though the lunch hour rush had ended, Sandra still leaned forward and said in a hushed voice, "I'm not one hundred percent sure yet — the Brotherhood delves deep into a lot of forgotten history for their spells — but this is my best guess. Oh, and before I forget, one other thing that might be important. One of the books I needed was missing."

"Somebody checked it out?"

"You don't really check books out of Haven House."

"You did."

"Not really. We can talk about that another time. The thing is that I've never known those witches to lose track of a book. Any book. It could be nothing — they are getting older — but I thought you should know. As for the spell — the Brotherhood failed to summon and control an inhuman spirit —"

"That was because of us," Max said around a mouthful of food.

"Well, they're still trying to achieve the same goal. Just a different tactic. They want power over all the witches. We know that. From what I can tell, best guess is this spell appears to be some kind of battery for storing magic energy. They trapped a soul — Samson Price — and they are siphoning off his energy. It's like how witchcraft essentially siphons off Nature's energy and uses it; they are doing the same but with the soul they pulled. I think that's why the spell was still there in the warehouse. It's continuing to pull off Price's energy and store it up."

"I thought that was a crazy risk for them — leaving Ashley's body and that spell to be found — but if they have to in order to get the energy they need, then it makes an ugly sort of sense."

"If it works, we may see more kidnapping-murders occurring. They'll need to cast the spell over and over until they have enough power to take on all the witches of North Carolina. Considering what Mr. Carroll acted like when we met him, I'm thinking he'll want to be more than just the leader of the Brotherhood. More than just the leader of magic in North Carolina. Once he's got the state under control, why not go for the whole country? Once you have that, why not go for another country? I mean I know world domination sounds a bit out there, but if the spell works, I don't see what would stop him."

Max swallowed his food, digesting Sandra's information as much as his sandwich. "That's a big *if,* isn't it?"

"Seems to be working for the moment. Maybe it's not that big an *if* after all."

"But to go from that to world domination — I'm not doubting, I'm trying to see if that's a real possibility for him."

"He struck me as the kind of man who is never satisfied. He'll always want more. Whether he'll be able to siphon enough souls to gain the power needed for a doomsday scenario, I haven't a clue. What he's doing has only been attempted a handful of times in nearly seven centuries. Nobody's too clear on how much power you get from a soul. And then, of course, he has to be able to use the power."

"Without killing himself."

"Yeah, there's that. Though, he's shown himself more than capable of sacrificing others. I'm sure he'll find a way to test out his abilities without risking his own life too much."

Wiping his mouth and taking a drink of water, Max thought about Mr. Carroll. The small, heavyset man who played the part of the genteel Southern gentleman yet had raw, brutal, ambitious blood coursing through every vein of his body. "This is a serious threat, but it doesn't sound like anything he can achieve today. We have time to learn more, plan a counter attack, find some way to disrupt what he's doing. Or do you already know how we break the spell? Is that why we told Brenda to come out here?"

As she spoke, Sandra scrolled through the notes on her phone. "Because Samson Price had already moved — as I understand what I'm reading — he's already transformed."

"Which is?"

"When we move on, our soul and ghostly body are separated. He's a soul, a human spirit, no longer part of our existence. That didn't happen to Drummond because he left before that process could take place. He chose to come back and stay connected to his ghostly body."

Max shivered. "It's hard to think of what Drummond is as a body. But I understand."

"The Brotherhood had to have chosen Samson Price for a reason. The spell requires the caster to name a specific soul."

"What's so special about Samson Price?"

"Exactly. I think there is still a strong connection between Price and our world. He must have been involved in something to do with the occult or magic. That connection made him a more desirable target for the Brotherhood. He would be easier to pull back to our reality and, assuming I'm right that there is a magic connection, he'll have more energy to siphon off in his soul. Whatever it is about Price that makes him valuable to the Brotherhood, we need to figure it out."

"And with that knowledge we can break the spell?"

Sandra picked up her fork and poked at her lunch. "Possibly."

"Since Brenda is connected to Price, you think she'll be needed for whatever spell you'll have to perform. Right?"

"I don't know. Maybe. Probably. But I figured, better to have her here and not need her than to need her and not have her. Until I know more, it's the best I've got right now."

"I learned a long time ago not to underestimate you. If you think this is the right track, then I'm all for it. Frankly, that's why we're in Hiddenite. When we finish our lunch, we're going to a museum to learn about the man Samson Price wanted us to learn about. Diamond Jim."

# Chapter 22

"I MANAGED TO FIND OUT a little before we left the Haven House Library," Max said as they settled the bill and strolled out to their car.

"Just call it Haven House."

"I'm not sure I can. It's a witch library, after all."

"I'm a witch, after all."

Pulling her in close, he kissed the side of her head. "My witch. That's different. And what does it matter what I call the place?"

"Because I use it, and I have to deal with the witches running it."

"You think they'll know if I call it something different?"

"You really want to find out?"

Max checked if she was joking. "So, it's Haven House?"

"Yup."

"I'll try to remember. Anyway, the museum we're going to was once the mansion of James Paul Lucas, aka Diamond Jim. The local legend is that the home was originally built in 1900 as a two-story Victorian by a young man smitten with his bride-to-be and intending to move in once they were married. But they had a huge fight, or several of them, and in the end, they never married. Diamond Jim — he got the name because he traveled all over the world as a diamond and gem importer — well, he bought the house. But he wanted more out of it, a third floor. Rather than simply build the floor atop the existing structure, he cut the building in half — horizontally — and had the original second floor with the roof lifted up on railroad jacks."

"Half a house?"

"Yeah. Crazy." They drove out of the parking lot down a street lined with homes. "They raised the floor only a few inches at a time and would put in something called *cribbing* which I think are massive versions of shims but I'll have to look it up. Little by little they kept raising half the house until wood posts could be inserted for support. Once high enough to build the new second floor, they got to work."

The mansion appeared on the right with no fanfare, no big signs, no massive museum parking. Just another house on the street. Granted, it was a three-story building with off-white siding, dark green trim, and rust-red roofing. It had numerous balconies, a gazebo painted to match the house, and a gravel drive that dipped down off the street and wrapped around the building. Standing proud amongst the everyday homes surrounding it, Max could imagine what the locals must have thought when Diamond Jim raised half his house to insert a new floor — it wasn't pretty. Then again, the man used local lumber and local labor. That probably won them over. Yeah, they welcomed him and his money as a great, somewhat eccentric, addition to the town.

Parking around the back, Max and Sandra found Brenda smoking a cigarette and pacing. She offered a short wave. By the time Max exited the car, she had stubbed out the cigarette and hugged Sandra.

"Thank you for calling me," Brenda said. "I was going to go batty cooped up in my apartment with a cop and nothing to do but think about that poor girl."

Max said, "Don't thank us yet. This could all be a waste of time."

"You don't believe that. Even if you do, I'm happier trying than not."

"I guess it does feel better to do something, anything. How'd you get away from Osorio, anyway?"

Brenda chuckled. "Told him I had to get more smokes. I think he's too shook up to notice, anyway."

"That might turn into a problem. He doesn't let things go."

Sandra said, "We'll have to deal with him later. Right now, we're here. Let's get started."

The entrance was through a door that long ago led to the

basement or cold cellar. Max stepped into a gift shop with a staircase to his left and a small desk in front of him. A young man wearing a museum T-shirt welcomed them, said they had to wear a mask inside the building, and added that donations were welcome. Also, the tour guide was sick, but since nobody had come into the building all day, he would let them roam free throughout the guided section as well as the normal self-guided section — just don't tell.

Max thanked the man and promised to donate when they left. They climbed to the third floor which started the winding path through the house all the way back down, and Max's body tingled. Windows lined both sides of the hall, blasting light everywhere. This had to be the right place. Not because of the windows, but rather because of what they revealed.

"It's like a witch lived here," Sandra said.

Max agreed. Every inch of the house was loaded with collected items. The initial hallway with salmon carpeting and wide, dark wood trims boasted two large and detailed doll houses. At the far end, they stepped into a narrow room with glass cases on either side — each one filled with dolls. Classic dolls dressed for an evening ball and others dressed for weddings. One shelf had a complete set of old Disney dolls from *Snow White and the Seven Dwarves* including all of the title characters, Prince Charming, and the witch. The next room continued the doll extravaganza with figures from all over the world, some puppets, and a few marionettes.

Max tried to hold back a shiver. "One old doll is creepy enough. But two rooms filled with the things — I'm glad it's not the witching hour right now."

"Amen to that," Brenda said.

Sandra's eyes roved the shelves with an alert sense of caution. "Be careful, anyway. I can feel something strange here."

The second floor had several rooms that were converted into art galleries showcasing local talent as well as gifted individuals from across the country. A few doors over, Max entered an empty room lined with photographs on the walls.

"This is what I wanted to find," he said, reading over the

information provided with each photo.

Dating from 1912 to 1952, the photos ranged in subject from portraits of Diamond Jim, his family, and his dog to several rooms of the original house, his enormous collections, and some of his hunting exploits. The first pictures to draw Max in were nothing more than rooms in the house filled with the many things James Lucas had gathered over the years.

One photo showed his collection of political convention buttons, clocks and pocket watches, several assorted chairs, and various owl figurines. Another presented a line of alcohol bottles, mostly filled, running along a fireplace mantle despite Prohibition being in effect at the time. There were also various bits of horse-riding tack such as saddles, bridles, stirrups, and more. A large sombrero hung on the door — supposedly once owned by Pancho Villa. Still more photos depicted rooms filled with boxing gloves and battle helmets from various people — some famous, some not. Several taxidermized animals looked out from dead eyes. And weapons everywhere — percussion cap muzzle loaders, World War I German service rifles, a Sharp's repeating carbine, a Smith & Wesson Model 3 from the Spanish American War, a Civil War Remington revolver, and many more.

Max could not tell if Diamond Jim had been a discerning collector seeking specific finds or if he had been a hoarder, grabbing hold of everything he stumbled across on his travels. The other pictures were equally of interest — particularly the portraits of J. P. Lucas himself. Each one seemed to be a different man, yet the descriptions promised they all were of Mr. Lucas. In one, he dressed like a university student. In another, like a dapper gangster.

Between the limited research he had time to do, what he had seen of the house so far, and this photo room, Max had put together an idea of Diamond Jim that may have hit close to the mark. The man had been full of life. An adventurer who loved to keep hold of pieces of his experiences as if they were memories themselves. The more places he visited, the more friends he made. In turn, they provided him with more objects to remember wonderful times.

He struck Max as an intelligent man. Well read. Indeed, his eccentricities led to some fascinating and forward-thinking design choices in his home. The building had an indoor water system — quite fancy in the early-1900s — as well as a telephone and fire extinguisher system. A power generator provided all of the home's electricity.

"Oh, hello," Sandra said, looking toward the doorway.

Max didn't see anybody — which usually meant one thing. "Do we have a ghost with us?"

"We do."

Brenda beamed as she gazed in the same direction as the others. "Really? You people are amazing. I've never encountered much paranormal stuff for real in my life. Spent most of the time talking in groups like the Peepers and wondering if that door movement or that rusty whine in the hall is a ghost, yet here we go again. Another ghost."

"A man. He's got a huge beard and a thick accent. Big guy with big muscles. He's laughing at my description. Says he ate well and worked hard his whole life."

"Did he die in this house?"

"He says *No.*" She listened a moment. "His name is Frank Card. He lived in this town his whole life, and he likes to come here because he helped work on the raising of the old second floor to make the new one. Says he'd never seen anything like it. Amazed him." She listened more. "He wants us to follow him."

Max gestured to the door. "Lead the way."

Following Sandra following a ghost, he had an unnerving thought. *Brenda's right about that — here we go again.* Even with the daylight drifting onward, even when Sandra showed no signs of discomfort around this particular ghost, Max could not help but be alarmed. He had no clue what to expect, and no information to judge by except that Sandra appeared fine with it all. That would have to be enough.

They came upon a door with a sign designating the part beyond for guided tours only. Sandra did not hesitate to step through. Max and Brenda followed.

This section of the house preserved the original design and

décor from Diamond Jim's time. Hardwood floors, a few with old but intricate rugs, accentuated their footsteps. The level of collected clutter rose exponentially. Every surface — every table, every bench, every bureau, even a few chairs — all weighed down by objects of memory. Kitchen supplies, small figurines, tea sets, fine China, books, blankets. And where no suitable surface existed, one had been installed — a ledge built over the doorway, a wall recessed to create shelving.

Max paused to pull back the corner of one floor rug. Nothing. No casting circles. No witch symbols. Just wood floor. He set the corner back before catching up with Sandra and her ghost.

They entered one particular room, presumably Diamond Jim's corner office, where they found a desk suitable for such a gregarious man and a lamp with a tasseled shade off to the side. Small antlers had been set on the fireplace mantel and above on the wall, mounted upon an oval-shaped base, two animal heads — a wolf and a bear — glared at the room with threat and disdain. Beneath one window, an old trunk acted like another table, and a figurine of an African man riding an elephant had been set on top.

"He's over there," Sandra said, indicating a wall covered in framed photographs. "He wants you to take a look."

"Me?" Max said.

"Frank says that he wants you to see what he looked like." Pressing closer in, she added, "I can see what he looks like, but I think the real reason he wants you over there is because he doesn't like dealing with women."

Max stepped closer like a soldier walking across a minefield. He didn't want to brush against or through the ghost let alone disturb any of the museum pieces. With a few encouraging words and the occasional *To your left, honey* or *Careful on your right*, Sandra guided him across the room.

Amongst the old black and white photos on the wall, Max noticed one that showed the new second floor being installed. A bizarre sight. Half of the house hovered several feet above the other half while laborers worked to get wood braces and supports in place. Another photo showed the finished product, and a third had all of the workers in two rows with Diamond Jim on one end standing in front of the house before the project had begun.

"Which one is Frank?" Max asked.

Sandra said, "He says he's five from the left in the back row."

Bending to get a closer look, Max counted it out and landed on a man with a thick beard that draped his broad chest, thin eyes that seemed trapped in a squint, and a wide frame built of hard work and toughened muscle. His round face stared into the camera with quiet confidence. "Okay, I think I found him."

"He says to keep looking."

"How about he just tells you what he wants me to see?"

Sandra looked around the room as if listening for the source of an odd sound. "He's gone."

"Gone?"

"He looked scared."

"Wonderful. A ghost brings us all the way to this room but is too scared to tell us why and then disappears. I feel like we're being set up, or at the least, pranked. I mean ..." Max stepped back, his eyes fixated on the photograph.

"I know that look. What did you find?"

Tapping a group of black men standing near Frank Card, Max set the photo on the table so Sandra and Brenda could see.

"Okay, I'm looking," Sandra said.

Immediately, Brenda pointed to the man standing next to Frank Card — a rugged face that had seen hard years. "Right there. That's Samson Price. I know it."

"That's how Price is connected to Diamond Jim Lucas." Max returned the photo to the wall. "He helped construct the new second floor of this house. And he used everything he had to get us out here."

Sandra said, "I think it's safe to assume that the thing which gives Price such a strong link to this world is in this building."

"Probably." Max stretched his back and rolled his neck. "It would've been nice if he had picked an OCD, minimalist neat-freak. If we could take one look at a room and see this thing sitting under glass in the middle, I would've been real happy."

Sandra lifted her gaze upwards. "I'm betting it's one of those spooky dolls up top."

"I doubt it," Brenda said. "Sorry. Not trying to tell you about your business, but the Samson Price that possessed me would find those dolls far scarier than us."

"He may not have had a choice about it."

"Could be one of the animal heads on the walls." Max sighed. "I'm not even sure where to begin. There's too much stuff in this house."

A thick, Southern voice with a cadence belonging to generations back spoke up. "Perhaps I may be of assistance with your inquiries."

"Crap," Max said. He recognized the voice right away. Mr. Carroll.

# Chapter 23

MR. CARROLL LEANED HIS HEAVY BODY on a walking stick. His stark white goatee gave definition to his face, while tinted, round glasses gave it character. Though a short man, he filled the room as if his bald head rubbed the ceiling.

Standing next to him, one of his followers — the one Max thought of as Punk Girl — brandished a handgun. She had buzzed white hair that stood out against her dark skin and wore classic punk styles — combat boots, chains for a belt, safety pin earrings, and several necklaces.

"I do believe," Mr. Carroll said, as if entertaining guests at his plantation on a summer day, "that I never properly introduced you to my associate. Mr. and Mrs. Porter, it is my pleasure to present you with Ms. Lydia Stokes. I'm afraid I am unacquainted with your lovely companion."

"I'm Brenda Byrd." She sounded far stronger than her shivering legs bumping against Max.

"Hello there, Ms. Brenda. I do apologize that you are here. Alas, I cannot postpone this evening's events. You will have to come along with us. Max, be a gracious gentleman and introduce Ms. Stokes to your friend."

Max held still, even as he thought that she would always be Punk Girl to him. At his side, Sandra's breathing shuddered, and that small sound caused him to raise his hands. A somber thought struck him.

"I suppose you killed the young guy downstairs running this place," he said.

"I should think by now you would know better of me. I would never be so crude or cruel unless absolutely necessary."

"Carving up Ashley Cortez was *absolutely necessary*, was it?"

Brenda gulped hard. "You did that?"

"Indeed." Mr. Carroll leveled his intense eyes on her. "A most unfortunate but necessary requirement for our greater aims. Ms. Stokes here is going to restrain you all, and I request your co-operation. Then we can get on with the matters at hand for which we are here." He took the handgun from Punk Girl, and she pulled out three plastic zip-tie cuffs. As she bound Max's hands behind his back, Mr. Carroll went on, "As for the young man who had to manage this museum by himself, you have no need to fear. He is incapacitated and tied up. That is all. We also took the precaution of locking the doors and putting the *Closed* sign in the window. It is essential that we have our privacy."

When Punk Girl finished cuffing Sandra and Brenda, she stepped out of view. A moment later she returned with a map of the house and a sledgehammer.

Max tried to swallow back the quaking in his jaw. Although this man did not behave like the lunatic version with the Brotherhood symbol carved in his chest that Max had encountered before, although this Mr. Carroll had the cold confidence of a man who had planned each step he would walk and found the path exactly as he had expected, he still maintained an aura of threat around him. Once again, Max promised to get out to the practice range and become competent with his handgun.

With a gentle incline of his head, Mr. Carroll said, "I owe you my gratitude. After our previous disagreements, my position as leader of the Brotherhood of the Rising has been tenuous. In fact, several of my colleagues did not share my optimism for this plan's outcome. But they failed to understand the key to today's victories."

He paused, and while Max wanted to withhold the gratification Mr. Carroll sought, he also wanted to keep the man talking. A talking man with a gun was not a shooting man with a gun. Max said, "Please, tell us. We'd love to know."

If Mr. Carroll detected sarcasm, he did not show it. "I should think the answer is obvious to a learned researcher like yourself."

"Ah. You studied us."

"Indeed. Know thy enemy." Mr. Carroll glanced over at the map. Punk Girl pointed to a position, and Mr. Carroll nodded. "Come with us, please. We have to begin our work."

Sandra jutted her jaw toward the handgun. "We don't get a choice, do we?"

"Sadly, no. But you will receive a close-up view of the Brotherhood's triumph."

Punk Girl led the way with Mr. Carroll bringing up the rear. He huffed as they wound back up the stairs to the second floor. Max considered making a move. He didn't fear the out-of-shape man too much, but he did worry about the handgun. Struggling for control of the weapon in the narrow confines of the stairwell might cause it to discharge. And if Sandra or Brenda should be in the bullet's path — no, he couldn't do that.

"I want to thank you all," Mr. Carroll said between hefty breaths, "for being so accommodating in a situation that I'm sure resounds quite stressful within you."

Max said, "Hate to make you feel less manly, but this is hardly the first time we've been held at gunpoint. Or tied up, for that matter."

Brenda muttered, "It sure is my first time."

"Besides," Sandra said, forcing a tinge of amusement into her tone, "we'd like to know what you're up to. If we've learned one thing over the years, it's that people like you don't want their exploits to be anonymous. You love an audience."

With a slow, dry laugh that lived between humor and threat, Mr. Carroll said, "Oh, you can rest assured, I will not succumb to such baiting. However, in this unique circumstance, I will eventually reveal what you want to know. After all, everything that is happening right now and everything that will happen in the hours to come is a direct result of the Porter Agency's actions."

Stopping in the middle of the main hallway, Punk Girl pointed to a section of wall. Mr. Carroll nodded. He then indicated for Max, Sandra, and Brenda to sit on the floor. As they obeyed, Punk Girl cleared away some of the photographs and moved a low table aside. From her coat pocket, she brought out a stud scanner and started marking where each wood stud began and ended on the wall.

"Now then, unless Ms. Stokes is extremely fortunate, this may take several attempts. So, permit me to be a little predictable, as Mrs. Porter here would have it, and I shall detail for you how your efforts are enabling this evening."

"If you think we're going to help you —"

"You already have. Until now, the Brotherhood had only a fragment of a letter with Samson Price's name on it. We knew he was involved with the emerald, of course, but by how much was another matter entirely."

Max said, "Emerald? From the mine?"

With two short strokes of his goatee, Mr. Carroll said, "I do believe you have no clue what you have gotten yourselves into."

Punk Girl gripped the sledgehammer, hauled it back, and slammed it into the wall. Several feet down, pictures rattled in place. Others dropped to the floor, the tinkling of shattered glass accompanying them. As she struck another blow against the wall, Mr. Carroll watched with an appreciative eye.

Turning back to Max and Sandra, he went on, "Like the Porter Agency, the Brotherhood values research and the knowledge that comes with it. Once the Brotherhood had agreed upon the next spell we wished to cast, we embarked upon our research in order to understand and locate all the necessary components."

Puffs of drywall dust and plaster fogged the air. Punk Girl paused to cough before resuming.

Sandra said, "You need an emerald for your spell?"

"Not simply any emerald. You see, we came across a few stories. Tall tales, really. But the grains of truth we could extract promised us that Mr. Samson Price had worked at the Hiddenite emerald mine. One day while working the sluices, he washed clean an unusual emerald — one that had already been shaped into a teardrop design. About the size of a man's palm, this special gem had not been cut by normal hands. No, my friends, it was by a man named Aldus Palmer — a member of the Brotherhood."

A sharp yank on the sledgehammer released it from the wall. Punk Girl leaned into the hole, and when she stepped back, she looked to Mr. Carroll and shook her head. He gestured several feet to the right. Shifting over, she began the process of removing pictures and pushing aside furniture once again.

Max had started to see how these separate pieces fit together. "The truth now — you didn't know about any of this, and you weren't looking into a spell. No, you were researching Aldus Palmer, weren't you? Perhaps seeking to know more about the history behind this organization you stole control over."

"I did no such thing. They had made an error when they questioned my admittance into the Brotherhood. I merely set them straight."

"That's how you found out about the emerald and its connection to Samson Price. Because of this Aldus Palmer."

"I should think that much was quite obvious. But our journey from choosing the spell, finding Aldus Palmer's connection, and thus Samson Price's — to my way of thinking, the order in which it occurred is all rather academic. Because, in the end, we are here. All of us. Now. Thanks to you."

Sandra said, "But you knew about Samson Price before we ever heard his name."

"Yet you see, dear sweet Sandra, a name is all we had. While the Brotherhood does understand the value of research, there are limits to our abilities. We learned Samson Price worked at the emerald mine in Hiddenite and that he had found the emerald. But that was it. All trace of him disappears. For all we knew, he sold the emerald off somewhere and left the country."

*Thunk. Thunk.* Punk Girl hammered a new hole in the wall.

"That's why you picked Samson Price to summon back." Sandra rose to her knees. "You didn't only want to siphon off the energy of a soul ripped from beyond, you wanted to interrogate him."

"That was my initial hope. Unfortunately, Mr. Price refused to be helpful, and I could think of no other way to persuade such a soul other than what we had already done."

Max lowered his head, feeling stupid for not having seen

some of this before. "You set us up. You left that spell with Ashley Cortez's body for us to find. One way or another, you expected us to hear about it — after all, at the worst, it would be discovered by the police and the story would definitely make the news. A couple shares or retweets, and we were bound to learn of it. Then, what? You've been following us?"

Mr. Carroll rocked on his feet, keeping his balance with the cane. "The Brotherhood is certainly gifted at the art of surveillance."

To his side, Max caught Brenda's head bobbing from one speaker to the next. He worried she might suffer an information overload. As welcoming to the idea of the supernatural as she had been in her life, this was far different. This wasn't a guess or a hope or a faithful belief. This was real. Far harder to accept or dismiss. And her life was threatened. That tended to make people unpredictable.

Sandra said, "What if we never took the case? We almost didn't."

"Why then," Mr. Carroll said with a wink, "I would have been forced to guarantee that you pursue the matter. Violently, if necessary. Thankfully, it did not come to that."

Watching Punk Girl check the new hole, finding it empty, and shifting down several more feet to start once more, Max did his best to set aside the adrenaline pumping hard through his body. Mr. Carroll's words served to remind Max how dangerous the man could be, but he also loved to be admired for his intelligence. As long as he continued talking, as long as Punk Girl kept breaking up the walls, that sledgehammer would not be turned upon either Max or Sandra or Brenda.

"It never occurred to you to check out this museum before?" Max asked.

Mr. Carroll shrugged. "Why should it? What connection could we possibly have found between a miner — a black man, at that — and a wealthy adventurer — a white man who owned the largest house in the entire town. In the 1930s? Only if James P. Lucas had been an owner of the emerald mine would we have connected the two. But you — you found the connection. You brought us to that picture."

"And you think Samson Price hid this precious emerald in the walls of the new second-floor. Why would he do that? Why wouldn't he try to sell it off and retire to some other country?"

Sandra answered this one. "Because Price knew. Somehow, he learned that this emerald was not natural, was not a valuable gem cut by skilled hands, was not a treasure, was not anything normal. What happened? Did a witch approach him? Did she explain to him that he held a stone capable of storing magic?"

"Quite close to the truth," Mr. Carroll said, as Punk Girl slammed through the wall once more. "A witch did visit that night, and at the behest of another miner, she infused the gem with its magical properties. Aldus Palmer had intended to all long, but apparently, he was a bit of a gambler and lost the gem in a game of cards. At least, that is the story that's been handed down. The full truth? We shall most likely never know."

"Still quite a leap," Max said. "To go from not knowing what the man did with this gem touched by a witch to assuming that he hid it in here because he helped build this floor."

"I may have glossed over some of the finer details."

Max leaned toward Brenda. "That's his way of saying he lied."

"An omission, nothing more. You see, this witch left behind some writings and ramblings of her life."

"You stole that from Haven House," Sandra said.

"Well, I hardly expected the witches of Haven House to allow us to take those books for our own purposes. Be that as it may, we acquired this witch's diary, labored hard to decipher its mysteries, and learned that Mr. Samson Price feared what her spell might do to him and his family, and he further feared what it might do to Mr. Lucas and his family as well. But he also wondered if perhaps the whole thing was nonsense — witches and magic — so he wanted to make sure the valuable gem was in a location he could reacquire it should that be the correct course. Apparently, he thought hiding it in these walls was the best choice available to him."

Punk Girl had reached the end of the hall and still no emerald. A shift came over Mr. Carroll. His shoulders lowered, his brow tightened, and his Southern gentleman grin soured. He gazed across his prisoners as if weighing his next words.

At length, he said, "It appears we were mistaken in our supposition that the emerald had to be in these walls. That is not to say the gem is not within the walls of this house. Only that it is not in the obvious and most practical location. Sadly, I do not have endless hours in which to properly search the premises. I'm afraid I have no choice but to call upon the Porter Agency one final time. Between all I have shared with you and whatever undoubtedly brilliant research you have already performed, I believe you can find the emerald for us. If you put your mind to it."

"You're joking," Max said, not a trace of amusement in his voice. "Why would we even think of helping you?"

Mr. Carroll pointed his handgun at Sandra. "Because should you refuse, much as it would grieve me to do so, I shall put a bullet through your darling wife's head."

# Chapter 24

HEART RACING, BLOOD POUNDING through his veins, Max paced across the green carpeted gallery that had once been a large bedroom. Or perhaps a reading room. Open and airy, it had a narrow fireplace at one end and several windows lining the wall. Similar to the photograph room, this gallery lacked furniture with the exception of a Victorian-styled loveseat placed before the main attraction — a large, contemporary painting of sunflowers against a dark blue sky. Other paintings hung on the walls, each focused on variations of the color blue. A placard detailed the artist and her rather normal life. A photo of her showed a middle-aged woman in an average art studio.

Max tamped down the urge to throw up. The steady *thunks* from the hallway promised that Punk Girl continued destroying the walls, now starting upon the inner side. Each blow of the sledgehammer bashed through Max's nerves, shaking into his chest.

Mr. Carroll had freed Max's hands from the zip-ties and allowed him to have privacy in this gallery, but only because Sandra and Brenda remained in the hall. At gunpoint. For all his early bravado about having had guns pointed at them numerous times before, Max's anxiety ripped through his system, clouding his thoughts, and obscuring the task at hand.

If only Drummond were with them. He could pass through the walls of the house and find the emerald in minutes. *But he's not here.*

"Okay," Max said to himself and inhaled slow, long, and deep. "It's up to me."

He had to put himself in Samson Price's position. Think from that man's point of view. And most crucial of all — assume Mr.

Carroll lied about the details.

"Hurry, Mr. Porter," Mr. Carroll said from the hall.

"It's been two minutes, and your girlfriend is causing a racket. I need some peace to think."

"I'm afraid you will have to make do. I have to pursue all avenues. And if Ms. Stokes discovers the gem before you do, why then, I will no longer require your services."

No further explanation came, but Max did not need the threat spelled out. He closed his eyes and attempted once more to calm his mind, to think through the problem. Samson Price. The emerald.

It was the late-1930s. Samson Price, a black man, worked the Hiddenite emerald mine. If Mr. Carroll was to be believed, Price was sluicing at the time. That involved sitting at a long, angled trough with a steady stream of water flowing down. Large containers of dirt pulled from the mine and its river would be brought to the sluicers, and they would spend hours hunched over the trough, sifting water through mesh-covered, wood trays. The water washed away the dirt, leaving behind all the rocks, minerals, and gems. The trays were thick and heavy, the work strained the back and neck, and the unforgiving pace kept the men quiet and in constant pain.

Suffering through all of this, Samson came across an enormous emerald stone, cut like it belonged in a jewelry store, yet nobody noticed. Not even the miners on either side of him. He would have had to show no surprise, decide quickly to take it, slip it into his pocket, and continue on without drawing attention. Difficult but not impossible.

But no — Max had gone too far back. It didn't matter how the man had managed to get away with the gem. He had to have done so; otherwise, why would Mr. Carroll be tearing up the museum? Which meant that Max had to turn toward the days after getting the gem.

Price would have had to contact somebody if he wanted his payday. What little Max knew about Price suggested the man didn't have a fence on retainer. He didn't socialize in criminal circles nor did he show any interest in witchcraft or the paranormal. In fact, Samson Price was a hard-working miner, a family man, and a regular churchgoer. He probably felt guilty about taking the emerald, and if not for the Great Depression, he might never have been tempted.

Then there was this witch. How did she get involved? Max did not believe Mr. Carroll's story, so where did that leave him? Perhaps the emerald had been found, cut, and imbued with magic long before it ever reached Price's hands. Perhaps, he found it after it had been gambled away and discarded. If that were the case, then it seemed possible this witch already knew about the emerald. Maybe she belonged to a coven that had been involved with it the first time. Maybe they had worked with Aldus Palmer from the start. And a coven might sense the reappearance of their magic in the world.

"Perhaps I'm just spinning my wheels," Max said, increasing his pace.

From the hall, Mr. Carroll said, "I do hope you're not trying to fashion an escape plan. I assure you that my trigger finger is far quicker than anything you could think up."

Flipping off the door to the hallway, Max stomped up and down the room with one hand clamped atop his head.

*Hold on.* If a witch had been involved in the manner that Mr. Carroll suggested, then she would have demanded payment. No witch works for free. Yet Mr. Carroll made no mention of a cost. And witch payments were no small matter. So, either the witch was a fabrication or the payment was so great that Mr. Carroll did not want to admit it.

Stopping in the middle of the room, Max's hand dropped to his chin as he tapped his pursed lips. The witch didn't matter. Aldus Palmer didn't matter. They had been involved in the creation of the emerald but not its hiding. If any of Mr. Carroll's version of events could be believed, then one more person existed in this scheme. Mr. Carroll had mentioned a friend of Samson Price, another miner. There was only one other miner involved that Max knew anything about — Frank Card.

That had to be right. It would be too much of a coincidence if Card's ghost happened to be haunting the very location in which Samson Price hid a valuable emerald stuffed with magic. Max rolled his eyes upward — *the things I have to think sometimes.*

"Mr. Porter?"

"Shut up already, I'm working on it."

"Now, now. There is no cause for such rudeness."

"Says the man threatening to kill my wife."

"I could kill your client instead."

"How about you turn that gun on yourself and save me a lot of time."

"You are still so full of vinegar. I only wanted to remind you that —"

Max whipped open the door to the hall and glowered at Mr. Carroll. "You need to decide what is more important to you — throwing your weight around to make me feel pressured or finding that emerald. The more I have to deal with your threats, the less time I have to think through this problem." To his side, Max caught Sandra's subtle grin. He wanted to ask Mr. Carroll for Sandra's help but knew that would not be permitted. Max would have to figure the way through this on his own. "Well? Which is a going to be?"

Even as he managed a subtle grin back to his love, he caught a strong look exchanged between Mr. Carroll and Punk Girl. Max feared he may have pushed too hard. Causing Mr. Carroll to lose face in front of his subordinates would not help the situation.

Raising his hands as he stepped back, Max said, "I'm sorry. This is all a bit stressful, and I didn't mean to lash out. I promise I am working on the problem. I will do my best."

Pressing the muzzle of his handgun against Sandra's back, Mr. Carroll said, "See that you do."

Max returned to the gallery, and as he closed the door behind him, he caught a wide-eyed gaze from Brenda. Despite all she had experienced, this was still a shock. Probably not the last of the day, either. Because he had an idea. In order for it to work, though, he had to hope that Drummond's behavior as a ghost was not atypical — starting with the fact that he could call upon Drummond whenever the ghost was within a few rooms of

Max's location.

"Frank?" Max gripped the back of the gallery's loveseat. "Frank Card, I can't see or hear you. But if you're near or in this room, if you are willing to talk with me, then please bang on the floor or the wall or move the furniture. Do something. Because Samson Price sent us here, and I think the two of you were friends."

He waited.

And waited.

And waited.

And *thump*

Just above a whisper, Max said, "Frank? Is that you?"

*thump*

He couldn't tell where the sound came from — the walls, the floor, within his own head. It seemed to come from all those places and none of them. He wanted to know which direction to look in, but being polite was not that important at the moment. "One thump for *yes* and two for *no*. Got it?"

*thump*

"Okay. Do you understand the situation? What's going on out in the hall?"

*thump*

"And am I right that you know about Samson Price and the emerald?"

*thump*

Max smacked his hand against the back of the chair. He came close to letting out a whoop but did not want to alert Mr. Carroll. Now, the big question. "Do you know where the emerald is?"

A short pause. Enough to cause Max several heart attacks. Then: *thump*

"That's wonderful. You're going to save some lives today. My wife, Sandra, she's the one who you talked with earlier. She can see you. All I need you to do is go out into the hall and talk with her. Let her know where the emerald is, and we can take it from there."

*thump thump*

Max closed his eyes and rolled his lips in to keep from

screaming. In a calm voice, one unable to stop shaking from the rage trembling under his skin, he said, "I don't know what it is you want from us, but you're going to have to talk with Sandra in order to make it known."

*thump thump*

"I don't have time to guess. And if we play twenty questions, it'll be more like a hundred-and-fifty questions." Quiet. Maybe Frank finally understood and had gone to talk with Sandra. But Max thought that would be wishful thinking. More likely, Frank floated nearby, waiting for Max to ask another yes/no question. This wasn't the first time Max had to play this game of thumps, but it felt like the most annoying and deadly. Damn, he really needed Drummond.

"Listen, Frank, I'm going to try to make this happen. I'll ask the questions, but I'm not sure what direction you want to go in. Do you need to talk to me about the emerald?"

Silence.

"Frank?"

A brush of cold.

"This won't work unless you thump around."

Max felt ice across his back. For a hopeful second, he thought that perhaps Frank paced the room. But he knew better. He knew the way a ghost could communicate with him directly. And as he braced himself for the shock of having a ghost stick its hand into his head, there was only time to utter the start of one word.

"Shi —"

Lightning jolted through Max's body, clenching all his muscles and gnashing his teeth against each other. The world thinned around him. It filtered into a pale blue. Floating before him, with an arm straight out and a hand plunged into his forehead, the ghost of Frank Card stared back. The burly man with his thick, overgrown beard had eyes that penetrated through the agony. But when he leaned forward and whispered, he sounded more like a doting mother. "Shush now."

The ghost withdrew its hand, and Max floundered backwards. But he did not fall. He did not hit the ground. Instead, the world froze and he floated, his heels skimming the surface of the carpeting. Gravity pulled him slower, and he had the time to think that this new sensation had to be Frank Card's doing.

Frank disappeared. But the pale light did not return to normal nor did his peaceful fall change into a bruising crash. Murky darkness formed at the edges of his sight and crept inward until he slipped away like falling asleep on a bus or train. He could feel the vibrations of his body in motion, yet his brain had closed him off into sleep.

*Except I'm not sleeping.* He noticed everything. Felt it all. As the images Frank had put into his brain began to appear, as Max understood he was not dreaming but watching another person's memory, he felt his eyes roll upward and his body release all of his clenched tension.

# Chapter 25

TWO IN THE MORNING. Frank Card and Samson Price stood outside the Lucas mansion. The new second floor had been coming along, but they still had plenty of work ahead. Both men had been drinking. They had been doing a lot of that lately. Ever since Samson found that emerald.

Max watched from nearby — and a bit up. As if he were the ghost observing a late-night exchange between two concerned friends. More intimate than watching a movie, more detached than if he had been in Card's head throughout. He wanted to ask Sandra how this was possible, what it took for a ghost to be able to perform this feat, yet he had to shove those thoughts aside. All the tangents his mind threatened to go on, the questions he wanted to ponder, all had to be suppressed — for now. This had to have cost Frank Card a lot. Max should not waste this insight into him, Price, or the emerald.

He tried to move in closer but discovered that unlike a ghost, he had no control over his position. *Guess this is more like a movie than I thought.* Max paid close attention, doing his best to observe and listen, to remember.

"I don't like this," Price said in a low voice despite being alone on an empty street in the middle of the night.

Card fiddled with the clasp on his denim overalls. "It's a little late for that. I've already put the gem in the house."

"Then get it back. We should both be able to get that thing whenever we need to. What if something happens to you?"

"Are you planning on something happening to me?"

"Don't talk stupid."

"I'm not the one with cold feet."

"It's just a matter of trust is all."

"Don't trust me now?" Card stepped across the street as if walking out on stage. "Have I done anything to make you doubt me?"

"It ain't like that. It's just — well, honestly, you have to admit that it's hard for a black man to trust a white man in any case."

"You have to admit I'm the only white man you can trust to even say that and not fear being strung up."

"But we're talking about an emerald that's gotta be worth a hell of a lot."

"And I'm your friend. Have I ever treated you less than a man? Have I ever done one thing against what I said I would do? No. You found that emerald sluicing, and it was rough and ugly. You brought it to me. Not any other white man. Not any of your colored friends, neither. You brought it to me. What did I do?"

Price answered with a fierce glare capturing the moonlight. "I'm not saying you did me wrong."

"But what did I do? I said I knew a guy who could cut that gem for us and that he wouldn't screw us over. Did I not say that? And did I not do that?"

"You did." Price stepped up to meet Card in the street. "You neglected to say that this Aldus Palmer had anything to do with a cult."

"I told you I ain't part of that. Look, I had read about this Brotherhood and went to a meeting to check it out. That's it. I thought it was going to be like a union thing, a chance to get us miners a break."

"You mean the white miners."

"But they were nothing to do with us. They were all into weird stuff that I wanted no part of. I met Aldus Palmer there, and he treated me well enough. He kept in touch with me over the years, reaching out and saying if I ever needed anything. That's how I knew him. That's all."

As Max continued to watch these two men argue in the dark, deserted street, he heard Frank's voice in his head. Not even really a voice — more like Frank planted knowledge inside Max's brain. Because the voice was a mix of both Frank and Max. It said that at the time Frank knew nothing about what had happened to the gem. Later, after, he learned that when Aldus Palmer cut that emerald into a beautiful teardrop gem worthy of a hefty sum, the man also called in a witch and had her curse the jewel. Frank never knew why. He thought it was some kind of experiment to see what spells the Brotherhood could handle. But that idea came decades later. At this moment, as far as he knew, the emerald was nothing more than an emerald.

"Look here," Price said, folding his arms. "The real problem is I got a need for whatever money I can get from selling that thing right now."

"I told you that it was going to take time. I ain't some city mobster with lots of connections on how to sell off stolen loot. If we go out there and make too much noise, we'll get caught, and then you won't get nothing."

"Well, if you ain't selling it right now, then you can go in that house and get it. We can put it someplace else, someplace we'll both have easy access to."

"Any place you and I can think of that we both have easy access to means other people have easy access as well. I'm telling you, the Lucas house is our best chance. Nobody's ever going to go looking in those walls. Especially because they'd think it's in the new walls, not the old ones. I can show you exactly where I put it. I'll show you right now, if you want."

"Lot of good that will do me. If I need to get it and you ain't around, you really think Mr. and Mrs. Lucas is going to let a worker like me walk in their house and start ripping up walls. I'll end up in jail, if I'm lucky. Probably won't be so lucky is more like it."

They continued to quarrel with such vehemence that neither man noticed the car racing down the street. The car had its lights off. It swerved and weaved. The driver clearly intoxicated.

From his vantage point floating in the air, Max watched as the car slammed into both men, careened off the road, and smashed into a tree. The ghosts of Samson and Frank flung out of their bodies, and Max wondered if that was a bit of artistic license on Frank's part. Even as the thought bounced in his head, Max was drawn toward the opening light in the sky. The night simply broke apart as if a door had slid aside and let the sun pour in. All that golden light fell upon Samson. The man's ghost gasped as he lifted upward and disappeared.

Frank tried to follow. Yet as his ghostly form rose into the night, a green noose stretched out from the first-floor office of the mansion and wrapped around him. It yanked him to the ground. He reached skyward, but the door slid shut, the light vanished, and only the night remained.

As the movie faded to black, the Max-Frank voice within said that over the years to come, Frank learned that because he had handled the gem last, the curse coupled to him. It bound him to that gem and thus to that mansion. Samson Price got to move on, but Frank Card would spend nearly ninety years roaming those old halls, watching the world pass by, and never feeling peace.

# Chapter 26

MAX EMERGED FROM THE GALLERY ROOM soaked in sweat and bumping the chewed-up walls as if he had been boxing a heavyweight champion. When he had awoken on the floor with acute soreness digging into his muscles, he discovered that the gentle fall — the movie-like experience of another man's memory — had seemed pleasant and safe but truly worked over his body with merciless power. The ghost of Frank Card had gone. Max couldn't feel the cold anymore, and looking across the hallway at his wife, he saw nothing in her eyes to suggest another ghost was in the room. He attempted a grin. He must have failed, probably looked halfway out of his mind, but he held her shoulders and nodded. "I found it."

Sandra pressed her cheek against his hand.

"Well done," Mr. Carroll said. "Take us to it, and we'll conclude our business here."

Punk Girl hefted the sledgehammer onto her shoulder and hauled Brenda to her feet. Helping Sandra stand, Max tried to find the energy within to argue, to push back, to fight or run, if necessary. But he wanted to curl up and go to sleep. He wanted a hot bath to soothe his weary bones and a stiff drink to settle his troubled mind.

"Please don't make me have to enforce my threat." Mr. Carroll raised his handgun. "Your wife is too lovely a flower and Ms. Brenda is too Southern a lady to suffer for your stubbornness."

Max said, "So impatient. I'm not stalling. I'm just exhausted."

"The faster you bring out that emerald, the sooner we can end this."

Not liking the sound of that, Max led the way back along the hall, down the stairs, and into the old office with the mounted animal heads and the photo of all the workers who created the miraculous second floor. Among them in the photo — Frank Card and Samson Price.

Max lifted the frame off the wall with care and set it on the desk behind him. When Punk Girl moved in, he put out his hand. "There's no need for brute force here. Besides, haven't you destroyed enough of a historical building for one night?"

She glanced back at Mr. Carroll, and he signaled that Max should be allowed to continue. Curling her lip, she jutted her head at him. A half-dozen comments rose in his mind, but he bit them back. Not a good idea to anger a woman with a sledgehammer.

Placing his ear close to the wall, he knocked on the wood and plaster. He started at the nail used to hang the photograph and worked to the left then right, up then down. When the tone changed, he made sure by knocking further around the area.

"Unless they used massively thick studs, I think you'll find your emerald right here." He pointed to a sharp letter opener on the table.

Punk Girl hesitated.

"Really?" he said. "You think I'm going to stab you? With your boss ready to shoot everybody? Come on, now."

Shaking her head, Punk Girl reached into her pocket and pulled out a short but deadly-looking blade. She set the sledgehammer down and bumped Max aside with her shoulder.

"Okay, okay. You can do the honors." He indicated where she should cut on the wall.

It didn't take long. Once she found the line, it led her the entire way. When she finished, she had outlined a square panel. Carefully, she dug in deeper until the outline became full cuts into the wall. A final time around the edges and the panel popped free. Inside, Frank Card had built a small ledge on which the emerald sat.

Even from over Punk Girl's shoulder, even without much knowledge of gems, Max could tell that the emerald looked exquisite. A stunning teardrop that must have fallen from the saddened eye of a giant. It looked wet as if recently shed, and when Punk Girl pulled it out, despite decades of dust caked across one side, light played off it, sending green sparkles onto the ceiling like a mystical planetarium show.

"Well, I'll be," Brenda said, hugging herself as if chilled by a ghost.

Mr. Carroll crouched over Punk Girl's hand, his face dazzled by the beautiful piece of art, and he stroked his goatee. An opportunity rose, and Max considered taking it. With both of their captors lost in the mesmerizing gemstone, he could make a move, snatch the handgun or grab the sledgehammer or simply take Sandra and Brenda and run. They might not even give chase now that they had the emerald in hand. But even as he weighed the possibilities, the moment vanished.

Mr. Carroll backed away and brandished the handgun once more. "A truly remarkable find. We all here have read old legends and histories of magical items before. We've all been down that path of obsession and devotion to a particular spell or ingredient or object. I believe it is the nature of the witch or those of us who invest in the lives of witches that we become this way. And yet, it has been my experience, and I imagine that it is similar for all in this room, that upon achieving those goals — finding that spell in some old grimoire, locating that one-of-a-kind ingredient after too many fruitless searches, holding that magical object that bore the weight of your thoughts for endless hours and days, if not years — that the results are inevitably underwhelming. There is satisfaction, of course, but the book is dusty and molding, the ingredient nothing more than a weed, the object smaller or less powerful than hoped. But this — look at it. Have you ever seen anything so richly beautiful, so full of potential, so worthy of the time and effort we have spent? It defies expectations. It is truly remarkable."

"I don't get it," Max said, receiving Mr. Carroll's furious glower. "Frank Card was cursed by this thing. That curse was laid upon it by Aldus Palmer — well, more specifically, Palmer brought in a witch to curse it. But you want to use it to store magical energy? How can it do that as well?"

Sandra lifted her eyes from the emerald. "Oh no."

"I wish that it could," Mr. Carroll said. "But the kinds of spells that would require stored energy siphoned off an unwilling spirit have proven to be far too difficult and even more costly. The last to explore such things beyond the books was Mr. Palmer."

Looking at all the faces in the room as her mind whirled, Sandra said, "The Brotherhood has known all along that it couldn't take control of the witches."

"That was certainly Mr. Palmer's conclusion. After numerous attempts at casting challenging and severe magic, he finally started to call in witches to cast various spells. He would observe them, try to learn from them, but spells of this nature require great precision and knowledge. He was bound to fail."

Max started to see where Sandra's thoughts had led. "He would still have to pay the witches."

"Indeed, he would. The curse upon this emerald cost him blood. A lot of it. Of course, not simply any blood would do, but that from someone he cherished. You see, to curse something so precious required the blood of someone equally precious. But I will not answer the question you will want to know. You are not of the Brotherhood, and thus, you do not deserve such an answer."

Sandra said, "It doesn't matter who he sacrificed. What matters is that he hated the witches for it."

"Very true. In fact, while not the first offense between witches and the Brotherhood, this marked the final one for us. The beginning of our disgust with witches and our desire to rule over them, to prevent such horrible things from happening again."

"How noble of you." The growl under Sandra's words gave Max a chill. She eyed Punk Girl a moment.

Clearing her throat, Brenda said, "I don't get it. If you believe what you're saying — heck, if you believe half of it all — then we should be on the same side. So, why'd you kill Ashley Cortez?"

Mr. Carroll's devilish grin flowed with satisfaction as if it brought him joy to relive the girl's death in his mind. "She was a descendant of a witch. It took far too long, but vengeance has always been a game of patience."

Sandra's eyes bolted wide, and she spun toward Max. "I got it wrong. This was never about gaining power over the witches. This is about revenge."

Frowning, Max said, "I know. I just heard him, too."

"Not that revenge. Not Palmer's against the witches." She turned toward Mr. Carroll before backing against Max. "This is about his revenge. Against us."

Mr. Carroll's mouth spread open, his sharp teeth catching a flash of emerald green. "Indeed."

# Chapter 27

THE DRIVE OVER to the emerald mine took only a few minutes, but they pressed against Max with wracking dread. After cutting Sandra and Brenda's zip-ties, Mr. Carroll had split Max from them, making sure that neither of the Porters dared disrupt the drive. Sandra drove their car with Brenda upfront and Mr. Carroll in the backseat holding his handgun. Max had to drive the other car, a rather nice BMW, while Punk Girl sat in the passenger seat holding her blade pointed at him. Even if the women could somehow escape, Max would be stabbed before he could lift a hand off the steering wheel. His stomach churned nearly as fast as his thoughts.

Punk Girl pointed to the entrance — a narrow driveway of rocks and dirt that forced Max to go slowly or else risk a flat tire. Barely enough room for a car passing the other way, but this late in the day, he did not expect that problem. With the sun lowering in the sky, the brush and trees created thicker walls on either side, filled with shadow, and his overworked mind conjured movement between every tree. Though they still had at least an hour before dusk, Max popped on the headlights to be safe. Last thing he wanted was to hit a pothole and jolt that knife into his side.

The road took a steep turn down and then entered a wide-open section of grass that had been marked out with wood stakes and twine. A parking lot, of sorts. Punk Girl gestured for Max to keep following the dirt road.

"Y'know," Max said, "I recall you talking last time we met. Something happen? You take a vow of silence?"

She moved the tip of her knife closer to his skin. He did not say another word.

After the parking lot, the foliage closed in again and the road dipped lower. Not far off, they came to an area Max thought of as basecamp. The road hit a T-junction with buildings off to the right. The left looked to be the way back out. A smaller dirt and grass parking lot greeted them across the road. Punk Girl indicated he was to park in there.

They got out, waited for the others, and then headed toward the collection of single-level, wood buildings. Some had corrugated metal on the sides or the roof, some looked unused for anything but storage. The buildings surrounded a central courtyard of dirt reminding Max of summer camp.

Except this place was empty. Probably closed on Sundays — the Lord's day off. Yet the folks at The Yellow Deli worked and they were the religious group. There never seemed to be an easy balance between the Lord and commerce.

With Punk Girl in the lead once more and Mr. Carroll at the back, Max and Sandra clasped hands as if on a romantic stroll. The intense grip that passed between their fingers, however, denied them any emotion beyond fear. Each step forward brought them closer to whatever Mr. Carroll had planned, and Max had no desire to find out.

Brenda walked next to Sandra and wore a blank stare. She was lucky to manage that much. Most people would be blubbering for their lives or laughing madly at the idea of ghosts and a magic emerald. To Max, a stunned stupor looked like a blessing.

At least he could glean one bit of good news — the Brotherhood's idea of revenge did not involve outright murder. After all, Mr. Carroll could have shot them several times over. Whatever he intended to do, it was not an execution.

But that good news only went so far. After all, not being shot in the head didn't preclude Mr. Carroll from killing them in a slower more painful manner.

As they headed through the camp, the ground on the left dropped to a long, open building — a small office where people visiting for the day could purchase their tickets alongside the sluicing area. It stretched downward with two long wooden troughs running through. In the middle, between these troughs, a dirt section sunk a foot or so. Plastic buckets had been stacked all the way down, each the kind for holding gallons of paint and each now containing dirt. Water rushed through the troughs and on the outside lane of each one, a wood bench ran the entire length of the sluice. Red clay and dirt caked every surface.

Visitors could purchase a bucket, sit at the sluice, and use a wooden box with a mesh bottom to sieve through the dirt. According to one of the hand-painted signs nailed to a support post, each bucket's dirt came from the mine and would be full of various types of gems — amethyst, quartz, onyx, and such. Mostly semi-precious finds. It was possible, however, to nab the good stuff, too. Even emeralds.

Max gazed along the sluicing area and tried to imagine it from nearly a century ago. Electric lights, maybe, but they would have been dimmer and strung along from post to post. Both sluices would have big men hunched over, sifting and sifting, tossing worthless rocks aside and putting all the valuable ones in bins waiting in the sunken section. The water would not be on a mechanical pump, forever recycled in a non-stop loop, but rather — what? He had no idea how these things once operated.

"Hard to believe it all started here," he said.

Mr. Carroll snickered. "It didn't. This is set up for the tourists. The original sluices, the ones that Samson Price had once used, most likely have been gone for quite a number of decades now. Of course, there's a slight possibility that the new facility is roughly in the same location, but I wouldn't be trusting that as fact."

Beyond the small grove of buildings, they continued downhill, following a dirt trail through the woods. A wide stream blocked their way, but four concrete slabs formed makeshift stepping stones across. Once on the other side, they followed the path which paralleled the stream.

On the left, a yellow, plastic chain had been strung between trees, cordoning off the woods and silently asking tourists not to wander. From all the piles of little stones everywhere, and from the price list at the office, Max guessed that people could stop at any point along the stream to jump in and start sifting for gems.

The sluicing area was for those who didn't want to get their feet wet.

It should have looked beautiful with the sun turning gold and red in the sky and the air filtered fresh by all the foliage, but Max found little beauty as each step brought them deeper into the depths of Mr. Carroll's revenge. What that entailed, what sick ideas the man planned to enact, Max had no idea. And not knowing only made the dread worse.

He thought about Ashley Cortez and what the Brotherhood had done to her. Blood magic preferred the freshest sources. It was possible — probable, even — that Ashley was alive through the beginning of the spell. She would have seen them gut her and remove some of her innards. Hopefully, she passed out or died shortly after.

And what of the others? Max and Sandra had witnessed the Brotherhood's ruthlessness before. They murdered two paranormal researchers to cast a bastardized version of an ancient spell in hopes of summoning an inhuman spirit.

"Right here will do quite nicely," Mr. Carroll said.

Max could see no difference between this section of the stream and any other, but Punk Girl tied Brenda's hands behind the trunk of a small tree before escorting Sandra to the bank and shoving her to her knees. With a small gesture, Mr. Carroll ordered Max to follow as he carefully placed one foot on a stone, then another, until he reached a wide, flat rock taking up the center of the stream. Water broke around the rock in two fast-moving rivulets. Gurgling as they dropped behind, they merged with each other and slowed into the next section of stream.

"Kindly stand on the edge. I need this space clear." Mr. Carroll didn't bother training his handgun on Max. No need. With Sandra held by Punk Girl, with that vicious knife scratching the side of Sandra's neck, Max had no choices. Not yet, anyway.

He took one step back to a small ledge on the rock. The water swirled beneath him, and though not deep, he noticed the streambed had jagged stones and slick ones covering the bottom. If he walked — heck, if he tried to run through the stream — chances were he would fall. While not fatal, he would certainly get banged up. Now that he thought about it, with all those jutting rock edges, a fall at the wrong angle could very well be fatal. There would be no heroic leap to Sandra's rescue.

Using a thick chunk of chalk, Mr. Carroll outlined the beginnings of a spell. Not surprisingly, he started with a triangle — a violent shape in witchcraft, one reserved for dangerous spells. He then drew a circle at each point of the triangle. Also, not surprising. Max had seen this design before. Twice. Both times due to the Brotherhood. Mr. Carroll formed a smaller triangle within the first one. Finally, and quite surprisingly, he drew a square in the center of the second triangle.

Max looked to Sandra. A square? What did that mean? She shrugged, but he couldn't be sure she could see enough of the design from her position.

Despite her wet eyes, Brenda said in a reasonable tone, "Forgive me for interrupting, but this still doesn't make much sense."

Mr. Carroll snorted. "You may not believe any of this now, but soon, you will witness that magic is true and real."

"Oh, I know that already. You don't call on the Porters unless you already know that much. No, sir, what doesn't make sense is you leaving bodies and crimes in your wake. What good is all this magic, if you're going to end up in jail?"

*Nice try,* Max thought, *but this man is far beyond logic and reason.*

Standing back, Mr. Carroll looked over his work, tracing it in his mind, clearly making sure each line had been set correctly. "Some groups have contacts within the police to protect against such consequences. Some risks are worth taking. The Porters have opposed the Brotherhood at every step. Initially, it was understandable. We did not begin our relationship on the friendliest of terms."

Max said, "You offered up me and my wife to be possessed by an inhuman spirit. That's a bit more than unfriendly."

"Granted. Under those circumstances — from our point of view — we had few options. But I say water under the bridge."

"Funny, I don't recall *revenge* being part of the whole *water under the bridge* idea."

"Perhaps it would be best if you did not consider the spell we are about to cast as vengeance of any kind. Rather, think on it as a form of punishment for your misbehavior. Now, I know that your past deeds came out of good intentions — you did not know the full truth of the Brotherhood's mission — and for that reason, we have decided not to end your lives. You see, Ms. Brenda, they deserve fair justice."

"Gee," Max said, "how kind of you. Here I thought you planned to kill us, disembowel us, and use our blood for whatever spell you're planning."

"No need. We still have plenty of blood from Ms. Cortez."

Pausing to pull out a silk handkerchief and pat the perspiration off his bald head, Mr. Carroll gazed up and down the stream. Mosquitoes dashed about while clouds of gnats formed at odd intervals along the water. The air grew colder as the sun offered less and less light.

"I'd say we best hurry along." Mr. Carroll dug into his coat pocket and produced a child's plastic cup with a spill-proof top. After unscrewing the top, he pulled a thin paintbrush from another pocket. He dipped the paintbrush in, and when he brought it out, Max saw it covered in thick, dark crimson — Ashley Cortez's blood. Mr. Carroll squatted near the top of his spell and traced the chalk lines, turning them dark red.

Max peeked over at Sandra. If she worked on an escape plan, he could not tell. Perhaps her mind had blanked as much as his. Only Brenda thought clear enough to offer a cogent debate, but she lacked a real understanding of the situation to help. Which brought Max back to his own empty head. But even when he had an idea, no matter what course of action he thought of, the end result was always Punk Girl slitting open Sandra's neck and gutting Brenda. They were simply too far away.

Standing up to readjust before painting the next section, Mr. Carroll said, "I do understand that this is not easy for you. Consequences rarely are. But you have stood in the way of this world's safety for too long."

A loud bark of laughter ripped from Max's throat. "Excuse me? We're the only ones out here trying to stop all of you crazies from ruining everything while you play with forces you don't understand."

Mr. Carroll's brow tightened downward. "Now, that is remarkably funny. A real tickler. The idea that you think we're the crazy ones. Unbelievable. Tell me, now, have you ever stopped to consider what the Brotherhood's true aims are? Have you once given a moment to not assume the worst about us?"

"There's nothing noble in a power grab."

"You have dealt with witches for too long, or perhaps your association with your wife has warped your understanding of the true villains. Witches and their like are the ones who seek the power. They are the ones who attempt to use forces beyond their understanding. But the Brotherhood seeks to stop all of that."

"You're a bunch of witch hunters now?"

"That approach is too small. Taking out one witch here, another there — it's a good strategy to protect a home or maybe even a village. But the Brotherhood wants to stop all of the witches. Not a select few. If we can take control of magic in North Carolina, then we essentially end its misuse in the state. From there, we can grow. Until the very idea of witches becomes what most people currently believe it to be — a story, a myth, a fantasy."

As he spoke, Max looked to the opposite bank, to the surrounding rocks, to the trees — but wherever he looked, nothing could be used to help the situation.

Mr. Carroll returned to his painting. "That's what you have failed to grasp from the very start. You were brought to this state so a family could wield its power over witchcraft. The Hulls use witches and magic like tech giants use money — to control others and reshape their world. I suppose it is to be expected that you would not see how many times you have hurt your own goals. Protect North Carolina from witches? You? How many times did you enable Mother Hope? How many times have you bought trinkets from witches? Books or spells or mojo bags or such? You financed them with the absurd notion that you were somehow fighting them."

"But not you, huh?"

"Oh, I admit that on one occasion or another, the Brotherhood has been forced into dealing with these unsavory types, but it was always a means to an end. Nothing more. Our true goals remain intact — to take over, then squash the use of magic. To protect the citizens of this fine state, and as we grow, to protect those beyond."

"It's a nice story. I'm sure it makes you feel warm and fuzzy about murdering people. But it's a lie. All your talk about protecting is nothing more than spin. You want to be judge and jury and executioner."

"I told you we are not here to kill you."

"Right. Just punish us. I'm guessing this spell is your justice?"

Mr. Carroll finished the last line, stood, and tossed the cup of blood into the water. He rubbed his back. "You are charged with a serious crime against humanity. Your actions have inhibited our ability to prevent magic and protect the populace. For that, I'm afraid the punishment is quite severe."

"Why am I not surprised?"

Concentrating on the lines of blood, Mr. Carroll took several deep breaths. He murmured something.

Sandra bowed her head. "He's started."

With a shrug, Max looked back at his wife. He came close to saying *I don't feel anything* when an unseen force gripped him by the shoulders and flung him down. His left hand slapped the stone hard but did not bounce away. It locked to the stone as if a clamp screwed his wrist tight. Catching his breath, he saw that his hand sat directly within the blood-painted square.

"No!" Sandra tried to jump to her feet, but Punk Girl shoved her back down.

"What?" Brenda cried out with a sharp break in her voice. Max knew that sound — the cracking of a person's shield. Though she had witnessed enough before to believe, she was only now seeing real depths of magic.

"There," Mr. Carroll said with a grim gaze. "Now we can begin. You may start to feel some stinging. That's part of the preparatory spell. You see, this bit of magic will wither your hand away to the bone so that my spell will have its fullest impact."

The *stinging* turned out to be agonizing flames lancing his palm and sending daggers up through his fingers. Max managed a chest-deep groan. Using his free hand, he wiped at the bloody lines of spellcasting. Nothing happened. Though still wet, the blood did not smear in the least.

"Do you know the tale of King Midas?" Mr. Carroll said, the mirth in his voice noting the futility of Max's efforts.

"Let him go," Sandra snarled.

With a condescending raise of his eyebrows, Mr. Carroll kept his attention on Max. "A learned gentleman like yourself, well, I'm sure you know the classic story. Anything the king touched turned to gold. Anything and everything. Goblets, chairs, food, his wife. In your case, the bones of your hands will be cursed to bring death upon all they touch. Obviously, you'll never be able to touch those you love again, and you'll have to be careful around all others, but even objects will suffer. Perhaps you'll get it in your mind to remove this hand, take a cleaver to it. When that cleaver hits the bone, it'll die — become a piece of metal neglected and ruined as if by centuries. It'll turn to dust."

Sweat dripped into Max's eye and blended with the tears running across the bridge of his nose. He tried to sit up, but the spell's grip on his wrist and the fire shooting through his fingers prevented such grandiose movements. He did, however, manage to breathe enough that he could speak — strained but speech nonetheless.

"Guess I'll have to join a demolition squad." He didn't feel half as brave as he sounded. He doubted Mr. Carroll was fooled.

"Your punishment, however, is more than all of that. Far more."

Brenda snapped her eyes tight. "This can't be real. This can't be real."

Sandra said, "Stop this. You don't know what you're doing."

He shot a perturbed glare at her. "I can assure you that I am well-versed in the spells I utilize." Then to Max: "Those who you destroy will be condemned to eternal wandering, never to rest, never to move on, never to find peace. And when you die, all of those who have suffered wrongfully because you accidently touched them — they'll be waiting."

"It won't work," Sandra said, wriggling to get free but barely able to move under Punk Girl's tight grip. "You've done the spell wrong."

Mr. Carroll burst to his feet and whirled around so fast, one foot splashed into the water. "Another word from you and I'll take away your ability to ever speak again. Just ask Ms. Stokes if I'm lying about that."

Both Max and Sandra lifted their gazes upon Punk Girl.

"Now, if you have nothing more to say? No? Good." From his inner-pocket, Mr. Carroll brought out the large emerald. "It is time to cast this spell."

# Chapter 28

FROM WHERE MAX LAY with his hand locked to the stone, he could only gaze upward and see a stark angle of Mr. Carroll. But it was enough. He watched Mr. Carroll raise the emerald overhead and heard an ecstatic rise in the man's voice. This was a triumph for him and his Brotherhood. He intended to savor every blessed second.

"Mother Earth is a mighty being," Mr. Carroll said like a travelling preacher. "Her bounty provides us life, and in death, her graciousness welcomes us back. From dust to dust, indeed. But too many play about upon her without ever understanding how much more she has to give. Not us, though. The Brotherhood of the Rising is here tonight beseeching Mother Earth to open her heart wider so that we may bring glory upon her."

"What a load of crap," Brenda said.

Max wanted to laugh, but he knew she only spoke because she had no other option to fight. He knew it because he had been through the same many times. If he could twist around to see her, to apologize for bringing her into this mess, he would.

As Mr. Carroll rambled on, Max tried to face Brenda, but he stopped on Sandra. She stared back, her eyes full of numerous emotions volleying between each other. He felt them all. They welled up from deep in his chest, matching her own. Love, fear, memory, loss — it was all they had left together. Soon, Mr. Carroll's curse would be cast and Max would never touch his love again. All their casual kisses in the halls, their morning hugs, holding her hand while strolling anywhere, and of course, the more intimate touching — all of it gone. Even leaning over her shoulder to smell her hair or listen to her breath, even the shuck of a shoulder as they laughed at a bad joke, even the simple act of passing the salt or washing dishes in the sink together — all of it gone. Soon a distance would form between them and they could do nothing to prevent it.

And that distance would grow beyond Sandra. His mother and the Sandwich Boys could no longer be touched. In fact, he would have to be careful not to let his hand so much as brush against anything. If Mr. Carroll spoke the truth about what this cursed hand could do to a cleaver, then it made sense that Max would not be able to touch a doorknob or a car steering wheel or a toilet lid. Heck, he might not even be able to rub his own nose or scratch an itch.

He felt the shudder in his chest before he knew how heavy his tears had become. With his free hand, Max reached out toward Sandra. *I love you*, he mouthed, his lungs unable to gain the air needed to speak.

She returned the most loving smile Max had ever witnessed. It radiated across the stream, cut through the dimming sky, and filled him with the same peaceful sense she always brought into his life, the same one that promised they would make it through whatever calamity they faced, the same one that guaranteed they would climb their mountains together. Despite the sharp blades cutting along his fingers from the inside, despite his anger at feeling so helpless, his cheeks rose as his mouth widened — and he laughed. Just a soft sound. A private moment shared between them. A testament to their endurance together.

Gaining intensity in his voice, Mr. Carroll went on, "The sacrifices of our brethren are not lost. Tonight, the fruition of all our labors begins."

"Hogwash," Brenda said.

Mr. Carroll paused to glower. Punk Girl stomped over to Brenda, and Max heard a hard slap across the face. When Punk Girl returned to Sandra, she gave a short nod.

Mr. Carroll continued, "With the success of this curse upon this man who has been a thorn amongst those who try to control the witches and those who play with magic, this man who has stood in the way of those who seek sanity and order in our world, tonight he will suffer for his actions."

Max wanted to protest this gross and misleading representation, but Mr. Carroll lowered his head and began mumbling several phrases over and over. Not knowing the language did not matter. All the preparations had ended. The speech had been meant to help build and then focus Mr. Carroll's energy. Now, the man pushed all that power into the ancient words that would cast the spell.

Sandra lowered her head, too — her eyes focused on the ground. Max followed her gaze. There, in the dirt at her knees, his indominable, unflinching, superior-to-all-other-witches wife had drawn a small casting circle with her finger.

She looked up. He understood. He had been wrong about Brenda's interruptions. She wasn't feeling useless. She had acted as a distraction for Sandra to draw the circle. But a casting circle so small made with tools as imprecise as one finger in the dirt could not create any spell more complex than the most basic. Even then, it might not behave as it should. Sandra's gaze warned Max to be ready. With a broader grin, he mouthed *I love you* again.

She blew him a kiss before turning her eyes to the ground. Whatever spell she had worked up, Max saw the fierce determination in her brow, the kind of inner-energy that scared him in other witches. Her fingers clutched at the dirt as her lips rattled off the words behind the spell.

Mr. Carroll leaned back, his arm shaking from holding the emerald overhead for so long. "Allow this vessel to channel your strength. Allow my words to guide your vengeance."

Snapping her head upward, Sandra said, "Never."

A blinding flash like lightning brightened the woods and reflected off the water. An audible gust of wind raced towards them, stirring up tiny tornadoes of leaves, twigs, and dirt. With the speed of a hurricane, the storm rushed through the area, flinging Punk Girl aside. The back of her head smacked a low tree branch, dropping her to the ground. She rolled, clutching her head, dazed and in pain. Brenda let out a surprised cry. In the next instant, the storm knocked Mr. Carroll off the rock and down into the stream. Max caught a glimpse of the man's head go under as he flailed, splashing about — still clinging to the emerald.

Another lightning flash and the storm ended. Sandra raced through the stream to reach Max. She wrapped her arms around him, kissed him, even as she tried to free his hand from the blood magic design. Wiping her eyes, she moved closer, examining Mr. Carroll's work.

Max couldn't help her. This required her expertise. But he could be the lookout. And from what he could see, both Mr. Carroll and Punk Girl were reviving quicker than he would have liked.

"Hurry," he said, knowing it was a stupid thing to say but unable to stop himself.

"I'm trying." Sandra stepped around the rock, slipping against a loose stone in the water. "There." She pointed to a series of squiggling lines near the top of the triangle. "The spells I found at Haven House used those symbols to regulate the energy coming in. At least, that's what I think it said. I'm still working on my ancient languages."

"Great, great. What do we do?"

"We need more of Ashley Cortez's blood, and I can try to rewrite what's here."

Punk Girl stumbled to her feet. She held the trunk of a nearby tree, bent over as if she might vomit, and wobbled in her efforts to stand still. Mr. Carroll sat in the stream, rubbing the side of his head, and breathing heavily.

With his free hand, Max touched Sandra's arm. "We don't have time."

"I can do this. With her blood, I know I can —"

"There is no more blood. Not here. You have to go."

"What? No. I'm not leaving you."

"You have to run. Get out of here. Find help."

"But —"

"They're going to be back up any moment. We can't argue. You have to go. For us. For PB and J."

She shook her head, sniffling, even as she looked from Mr.

Carroll to Punk Girl. Squeezing her arm tight, Max tried to find the words to send her to safety, as if he could cast a spell that would change her mind. But instead of running, she scrabbled across the rock, hugged him, and pressed her lips against his with the passion of all their years together concentrated into one moment.

"Whatever happens," she said, "I won't ever stop loving you."

He reached up and touched her cheek. He tried to memorize how she felt in his hand. With his throat thickening to match the stony lump in his chest, Max forced words out of his mouth: "Please, go. Run."

Crying, she nodded. One final kiss, and she broke away. He listened to her splashing off. He wanted to watch her, make her the last thing he ever saw should he die that night, but he clenched his eyes shut. No. He had to watch her or betray all they had built together. He forced his eyes open. Whatever would come, he would face it.

"Go on! Run!" Brenda said.

Sandra climbed up the rocky bank and onto the path with the yellow chain. She ran right by Punk Girl, shirking off the woman's half-hearted attempt to grab her.

But Mr. Carroll's voice boomed above Max. The heavy man had regained his senses and stood on the rock once more. "Ms. Stokes!"

Like a new recruit going through boot camp, Punk Girl snapped to attention but looked a bit sloppy — still unsteady from whacking her head on the tree. Mr. Carroll mimicked the motions of a baseball pitcher and hurled the handgun to the streambank. Before it hit the dirt, Punk Girl scrambled down to retrieve it.

It happened fast, yet to Max, everything took forever. Sandra ran, but he could still see her through the moonlit trees. Punk Girl stood on the path wielding the handgun. She yelled something. Then a flash of light. A loud crack in the air. Sandra ducked.

When she straightened, her hands were up. Max wanted her

to keep running — Punk Girl was still dazed enough that Sandra should have been able to get free. But then he saw Sandra's face and he knew. Punk Girl's words and warning shot were more than telling Sandra to stop. They were a threat and a promise. After all, the Brotherhood had Max and Brenda. If Sandra ran, Punk Girl guaranteed that Max would not leave the emerald mine merely cursed. Neither would Brenda. They would not leave at all.

Marching on the path, Punk Girl hastened over to Sandra. She wrenched Sandra's arm behind the back and forcibly brought her to the stream. But Sandra — she did not look ashamed or defiant or angry. She gazed at Max with the same warmth they shared moments before as if to say, *I couldn't leave you to die.* He returned a gentle nod. *I love you, too.*

Acting like a jovial grandpa, Mr. Carroll chuckled as he wiped water off his arms. "I am impressed with your persistence and your ability to cast that spell. Under the circumstances, a miniature storm from a hasty casting circle says a lot about your skills in witchcraft. You should be commended."

Sandra curled a lip. "Give me a moment, and I'll show you some real spells."

"I am quite sure that I'd rather not feel your witchy wrath. Now, you have had your chance at rebellion and you have failed. As impressed with you as I might be, I cannot excuse what you have done. Ms. Stokes has been injured, my spell has been interrupted, and I am rather fond of this suit which you have ruined."

"Can't say I'm sorry."

"I would like nothing more than to have such time as is necessary to see that all of you are punished, but I came here with one goal in mind, and I believe it best to focus on the punishment of Max. However, after seeing the way you act towards each other, I now also believe that in addition to this curse upon him, forcing him to watch your death, forcing him to mourn you while also trying to live a cursed life without you, would be an even greater punishment."

"Stop this," Max said. "Please. You've made it clear who

holds all the power. We'll step away. We'll close down the agency and, if you want, we'll even leave North Carolina. You have my word. We'll leave and you can fight with the witches all you want."

"But your wife is a witch, too. Besides, I cannot say that I trust your word for anything. No, your wife is going to die tonight, and there's nobody left to save you."

"Except me," a graveled voice said as a familiar fedora appeared out of the dark.

"Drummond!" Max cheered — a short burst of noise, really — and he saw his partner floating above the stream.

The ghost surveyed the situation. "One day apart and you're in this much of a mess — I swear, you'd both have died years ago if not for me." He formed skilled fists. "Okay. Let's end this Brotherhood nonsense."

Slashing across the air, Drummond headed straight at Punk Girl and Sandra. Of course. Max released a smile — the old ghost had to save the damsel first.

But when he came within five feet of Punk Girl, his pale body deflected in the air. He tried again, and once more was thwarted. Punk Girl stumbled back a step when he hit the solid air, but nothing more. As Max's smile dropped, Punk Girl's lifted.

Drummond frowned, whirled toward Mr. Carroll and bulleted for the man. Like before, his ghostly body hit something hard and angled off to the side. Mr. Carroll felt it and shook his head as if admonishing a simpleton.

"Your ghost can't help you," he said. "We made sure to bring wards with us."

Punk Girl fished out the pendant hanging from one of her necklaces — a piece of plywood cut into a pentagon and inscribed with a ghost ward. As Max turned his head back to Mr. Carroll, the man patted his right pants pocket.

"The Brotherhood is not made of fools. When we decide to have revenge, we study our targets well. So, yes, we know about your Mr. Drummond. We know that he was central to your prior success against us. As such, we came prepared." Lifting his head into the night, he said, "And to you, Mr. Drummond, I offer my thanks for joining us. We wanted to make sure our revenge encompassed all of the Porter Agency. Knowing that you are here and every bit as helpless as Max and Sandra, knowing you will be forced to witness the death of the lady and the cursing of the gentleman is the proverbial cherry on top. Sweet revenge, indeed."

# Chapter 29

AFTER A FEW MORE BLITZING RUNS, Drummond paused to rub his sore shoulder. Mr. Carroll held position on the rock, his arms folded, his feet set wide. Nobody spoke while this transpired — the constant attacks, the constant bouncing off the ward, the constant angry rubbing of an injured ghost body.

"If you would be so kind," Mr. Carroll said to Max during one respite, "please inform me when your ghost tires of this pointless exercise. I have a curse to create, and he will never get his cold hands upon me or my associate. I understand you think he can wear down our wards, but you are mistaken. These wards were made by a master of the craft. They will endure far more than you all can throw at them."

"Let's put that to the test." Drummond reset his hat and lowered his shoulder as he stared at Mr. Carroll like a bull locking in on a red cape. He rushed forward, slammed into the ward field, and careened off to the side.

Mr. Carroll's shoulder pushed back slightly as if given a playful shove. "Ah, I see. The hard-headed type. Very well. Ms. Stokes, kindly keep your watch on these people. I must proceed or we won't be finished until morning, and I do not wish to be that tired. Mr. Drummond, wherever you are, your friends already understand the rules but for your edification, I will make it clear once more — Ms. Stokes has a knife and a gun. She is not afraid to use them. If you, Ms. Sandra, or Ms. Brenda attempt to interfere with the casting of this spell, or should Max attempt an escape, I will kill Sandra. If it makes you feel useful, you may continue to break yourself against my ward. I have no fear of you."

Drummond readjusted his long coat. "I forgot how smarmy

that man is."

Despite the life-threatening situation, Max snorted a laugh. "*Smarmy?*"

"I've been around a long time. I pick up words here and there."

Sandra joined in, covering her face as her body bounced with laughter. "If you can't save us, at least, we'll die laughing."

Brenda frowned. "Why is any of this funny?"

Max and Sandra burst out more cackles.

Punk Girl looked to Mr. Carroll. The confusion on her face sent Max into a full bout of hysterics. Tears dribbled down his cheeks, and for once that day, they were not from sadness.

Waving Punk Girl back, Mr. Carroll grinned. "I take this laughter to mean that Mr. Drummond has said something amusing. Fine by me. Your joy will not hurt the spell one fraction."

To make his point clear, Mr. Carroll lifted his right hand high in the air. He held the emerald, of course, and as he lowered his head to stare at the blood magic symbols, Max felt the laughter wash away.

"Oh, Mother Earth," Mr. Carroll said, his voice stronger than before. More determined. "Hear me in this darkening hour."

Drummond flew across the stream and bashed up against the ward. He bounced back. Massaging his upper-arm, he shook his head. "This guy isn't fooling around. That is one tough ward, and I've been up against a lot of them."

"How did you find us?" Max asked.

"Not really the time for that."

"I can't move, Brenda's tied around a tree, you can't break that ward, and if Sandra attempts another spell, they'll outright murder her. About the only thing we can do is talk." Max paused, waiting for Mr. Carroll or Punk Girl to stop him. But Mr. Carroll continued murmuring his spell, lost deep in a meditative state, and Punk Girl kept her attention focused on making sure Sandra didn't do anything dangerous.

Drummond clicked his tongue before ramming into the ward again. His hat flew off, disappeared, and reappeared upon his head. "It took a while to pick through everything Price was trying to say, but I eventually got the idea of what happened. The key thing I heard was about the emerald. That and his talk about Hiddenite sent me this way."

"You knew about the emerald mine?" Sandra said.

"Doll, every schoolkid in Central and Western North Carolina visits that mine at some point. Teachers love it as a school trip. They were doing it long before I was born. Probably still doing it today."

Brenda said, "You're really talking to a ghost? Can it help us or are these wards really that strong?"

"Hold on," Max said. "You came here looking for the emerald?"

Drummond shrugged. "Yeah. And I found all of you."

"Surprise."

He took another run at the ward. No luck, but he let out a sharp grunt.

"Stop that," Sandra said. "You're only hurting yourself and wasting time."

Brenda said, "What's he doing?"

With a soft splash at the stream, Max said, "I don't think we're saving me from this, but you and the other witches can break the curse later. Right, hon?"

"No. Not right. Not at all. From what I saw painted on that rock, he's still working with old occult magic, stuff that predates formal witchcraft. Some of those symbols are not used anymore because they're unstable, and others because they're too stable — as in permanent."

"Hold on," Drummond said. "You're saying that —"

"If this spell is completed, it's possible that it can't be undone."

Slapping the rock he was bound to, Max said, "You didn't think to mention this before?"

"I only saw the spell a little bit ago. Then I was running for my life, then Drummond showed up — it's been a bit busy."

A jolt of energy lanced through Max's body. His limbs spread wide. Even his fingers splayed out. The hand locked to the spell twitched.

Max's eyes noticed a soft, green hue around his palm. Gazing upward, he saw the emerald had started to glow. A soft, pulsing glow.

But the skin on his hand remained. Mr. Carroll had said it would rot away into nothing, leaving behind only bone. Yet that hadn't happened. So far. Maybe Sandra was right.

"Hon, you said that Mr. Carroll's spell would fail. Why are we worried if he's not going to pull this off?"

"I was bluffing."

Punk Girl smirked.

Drummond swished away from Mr. Carroll and turned toward Sandra. "Tell me what to do, and I'll see it done. No matter what."

With more panic than Max wanted to hear, Brenda said, "This ain't right. Stop this. Get them to stop this."

Sandra covered her mouth, and her eyes narrowed with fear. A slight shake of the head. "I don't know. I don't think we can stop them."

Max's heart dropped. Not because of the curse that would soon be upon him — not entirely. Rather, he wished he could lift the burden he saw Sandra placing on her shoulders. And Drummond, too. Both of them would forever feel guilty for the Brotherhood's curse. Max wanted to tell them this wasn't their fault, but he knew that no matter what he said, they would still blame themselves. The fact that Sandra would be killed if they attempted anything didn't matter. The fact that those wards prevented Drummond from interfering in any significant way didn't matter. The facts didn't matter. Guilt didn't care about reality.

But then Sandra's face changed. She spotted something in the woods, and her brow lifted as she cocked her head. "What is that?"

Max saw nothing. He noticed Punk Girl searching the woods and also appearing to come up empty. But Drummond flew off in the direction Sandra watched. Something was there — but not something all people could see.

A ghost. That's what Sandra and Drummond usually could see that Max couldn't. But why would Sandra be unsure? Why would Drummond have to go off to inspect things? Unless …

Sandra said, "Is that?"

"Samson Price." Drummond drifted back. "What's left of him. Best guess I got — the Brotherhood's curse they're working on has to draw a lot of energy, right?"

"Which either forced him or pulled him here."

"Samson's here?" Brenda said. Then with a desperate cry: "I'm over here. Please, help us. We've tried to help you. Please."

Max peeked up at Mr. Carroll. If the man knew what was happening, he couldn't react. The spell demanded too much focus.

"Wait!" Drummond called out.

From the way he and Sandra turned their heads, Max guessed that Price darted over to Brenda. A moment later, he heard a snap, and Brenda walked into view, stepping onto the pathway with the yellow chain. She moved stiff-legged. Her left wrist flapped broken at the end of her arm, and the torn zip-tie clung to her skin. Her face was devoid of expression, and her eyes — cold, off, empty.

Punk Girl jumped back, aiming the handgun at Brenda. But then Sandra turned to face the pathway, and Punk Girl swung the handgun back on her. Sandra raised her hands again. But Brenda kept approaching, so Punk Girl turned her weapon back on Brenda. Back and forth she tried to keep both women under threat.

Too many targets. Too spread out. Max tried to sit up, tried to get a better view. A surge of energy zipped through his body. Not Mr. Carroll's cursed energy. This was different. This was a sensation charged with hope. Because Punk Girl's dilemma was their opening.

# Chapter 30

MR. CARROLL HUMMED A STEADY NOTE — low and satisfied. From Max's angle, the short man towered above, still holding the pulsing emerald overhead like the Statue of Liberty's torch. It would have been comical under other circumstances. But all possible humor hissed away as the emerald's color shifted. Darkened. With each pulse, it turned toward purple. The color of inhuman spirits. The color of mad, dangerous, uncontrollable supernatural energy.

Punk Girl waved her handgun between Sandra and Brenda. Max saw her from behind and had no clue what her face conveyed, but he could guess — anger, threat, a warning, and fear. While that combination kept Sandra from rushing forward and Drummond from attempting to break Punk Girl's ward, it did nothing to stop Brenda. Because Brenda had no control.

She stepped closer. A voice emerged from her body — Samson Price's cadence pushing through Brenda's vocal cords. "The emerald. I want. I need."

Max looked back to Mr. Carroll. The man had closed his eyes, lost in an ecstasy of his own making. The emerald had drained away all green.

This was it. With Punk Girl caught between multiple threats, and now Mr. Carroll high on the power surging into that emerald, this was Max's chance.

He curled his body around, twisting against his locked hand, and positioned his legs toward Mr. Carroll. The water temperature had dropped after the sun left, but Max had not noticed until he pulled his legs out of the stream. His hand throbbed. It didn't like the way Max had to maneuver.

No pausing. No moment to gather himself. The instant Max

reached the correct angle, he pulled in his leg and kicked out. Right for Mr. Carroll's shin. Max yelled, throwing every bit of energy within him down through his leg muscles, through his bones.

Mr. Carroll's humming ceased. Another kick. The man grunted. But he stood firm. He had no choice. From what Max had observed and what Sandra had said, he figured the spell had to be completed in its entirety to work. And once complete — he would never forget this part — it could not be broken.

Max kicked again. The pain registered on Mr. Carroll's face, but the man held his ground. He continued concentrating, continued holding the emerald up high, continued casting.

"No!" Sandra cried out.

Max slipped his next kick, scraping his knee on the rocks and missing Mr. Carroll entirely. He unraveled, relieving his hand a moment, and looked over at the bank. Punk Girl had figured out a solution to her problem. She had yanked Sandra over and put the gun to her head.

Before Max could shout an empty threat, a gruff voice said, "Stop right there. Drop the weapon."

Detective Jorge Osorio approached along the path. He had his handgun out, properly held, and trained on Punk Girl. His badge, though difficult to see even with strong moonlight, gave him a greater aura of authority.

"Well, well," Drummond said. "I knew having a good cop around would be helpful, but this is more than I could've asked for."

"Put the gun down," Osorio said, stepping between Brenda and everybody else. "Whatever this all is, it's over."

Punk Girl tightened her grip on Sandra's arm. As Brenda walked closer to the bank, Osorio moved with her.

Sandra said, "She doesn't speak."

"Well, she can hear, can't she?" Osorio took a firm stance, gripping his weapon with well-trained confidence. "Come on, lady. If you shoot that woman, I'll put a bullet in you. But you won't die. You'll go to jail for murder. Let her go, and things can turn a whole lot different. Look around you. The only one on your side is that nutjob praying on the rocks. He's not going to help you. Even if he wanted to, he can't reach you in time."

Brenda took another step forward, and Punk Girl dragged Sandra to intercept.

"Hey, hey, hey!" Osorio moved fast, but Brenda halted, seemingly to stare at the situation. To Punk Girl, he said, "You do that again, and it's over."

Swallowing hard, Max watched his wife hold her cool even as he unraveled inside. He couldn't do anything for her. Neither could Drummond.

Twisting back toward Mr. Carroll, Max said, "Partner, help me here."

Drummond tapped the brim of his hat and lowered his shoulder. "You thinking the same thing, huh? Can't help Sandra directly, but we can stop this bozo."

"On three. One … two … three!"

Max kicked hard as Drummond barreled into the ward. Mr. Carroll stumbled from the hit. The pulsing emerald skipped a beat.

"Again. One … two … three!"

They slammed in together. Mr. Carroll's left foot slipped into the water, but he stepped back into position and continued casting. The purple pulse grew heavier, angrier.

Max peered over his shoulder at Sandra. Seeing what happened to Mr. Carroll, a bright rage flushed across Punk Girl's face. She whipped her handgun toward Max, and that mistake set everybody in motion.

Sandra let her bodyweight drop her to the ground. The sudden tug knocked Punk Girl's aim off. She still managed a shot, but nobody would ever learn where that bullet went. Osorio's aim, however, hit perfect.

His bullet pierced her shoulder. She dropped her gun and opened her mouth in a silent, surprised cry. In the next second, Brenda leaped across the dirt, her arm wide to tackle Punk Girl.

"No," Sandra said. "Wait."

But Brenda ignored the warning. When she came in close, Punk Girl's ward reacted to Samson Price's presence. All of her momentum smashed back against her as she hit the ward wall. Brenda toppled onto her back, and though Max could not see anything, he noticed Sandra's eyes follow the empty space rising from Brenda and shooting upward — Samson Price had been knocked out of the woman.

Sandra pointed to Osorio. "Get that emerald."

With gratitude, Max watched as Osorio obeyed. The man knew enough to listen to those who understood more at the moment. He grabbed a set of handcuffs off his belt and tossed them to Sandra. Then he turned toward Mr. Carroll.

Back on her feet, Brenda's face locked in fuming anger. Whatever disorientation she suffered washed away in that tide of rage. She rushed the wounded Punk Girl once more, only this time, that ward would do no good.

"Come on," Max said to Drummond and pulled his foot back again. "Put everything you got left into this."

"You think I've been holding back?"

"I think that emerald is looking far too purple."

"Then shut up and count."

"One … two … three!"

Max screamed as he blasted his foot straight into Mr. Carroll's shin. He heard Drummond's pain-soaked howl as the ghost bashed against the ward. It was enough to send the short man flopping forward as his legs splayed back behind him.

He hit the stone with a loud grunt, his chin taking it hard. Blood stained his white goatee, and his eyes dazed. But more than the satisfaction of inflicting some pain, Max thrilled at the sight of Mr. Carroll's empty hands. He had lost the emerald.

Max heard Sandra yell. He snatched a glance over his shoulder to catch her smacking the side of Punk Girl's head. They had Punk Girl face down in the dirt, and both women straddled their enemy, using their combined weight to hold her still. Sandra wrestled to cuff the woman.

"I can get it for you," Drummond said to the air nearby. Max looked for any sign of Samson Price but saw nothing.

From beneath the stream, a dark pulsing purple rippled. Drummond soared over Mr. Carroll and plunged his hand into the water. Wincing before he even touched the emerald, he turned away from Max. He could hide his face but not his voice.

Touching the world of humans always caused pain to a ghost, but from Drummond's wretched scream, this was far worse. The waters around him bubbled as he pulled the gem out. He arched back, yet he could not yank it out fast. Something fought back.

With a deep howl, Drummond lifted the gem out of the stream. Not magical fighting but magical weight. Based on Drummond's behavior, Max guessed over a hundred pounds. No longer acting modest, the ghost used both hands to pull. Smoke wisped between his fingers while his mouth opened wide. He bellowed.

And dropped the emerald.

It plopped back under the stream.

"Don't," Drummond said to Price.

But then Max watched as the purple gem rose again. It moved slowly and shook under an unseen strain. With a splash, it returned to the streambed.

"Told you," Drummond groaned, holding his burned hands close and bending his body over. Max never understood how a ghost could heal, but then, he never understood a lot about ghosts.

With the hiss of opening a soda can, Max felt his wrist release from the stone. Unwilling to question a moment of good fortune, he rolled off into the chilly water. He must have looked cartoonish as he fumbled to his feet, splashing water everywhere, as he scrambled to the sloped edge of the bank. When he reached land — all of five steps — he flopped onto his back and cradled his hand.

Jorge Osorio patted Max on the shoulder as he walked by. "It's that glowing stone, right?"

"Leave it alone," Max said but knew he would be ignored.

Osorio headed straight for the purple light coming up from the streambed. Forcing his body to rise, Max got back on his feet. He yelled Osorio's name, shouted the word *Stop*, but Osorio pressed on. The emerald's Siren call lured the detective further in. Max splashed after him, but it was all over.

Accepting the reality of magic for the first time — fully accepting it without any dismissal — Osorio's world narrowed upon that swatch of purple beneath the babbling waters. He reached down into the cold, clasped the emerald in his right hand, and lifted it out. And for a fleeting second, a scant breath, Max thought it would be okay.

Osorio stared at the gem. Its purple glow reflected on his wide gaze. He even laughed. A child discovering Mother Nature.

Until the burn began. Osorio's eyes widened as his mouth dropped into a full-throated shriek. He tried to hurl the gem, but his fingers would not open. Not at first. On the third try, Max saw those fingers unfurl — and the emerald remained. Stuck to his skin. Searing the flesh. Sizzling.

As smoke belched off Osorio's palm, Max rushed over. He wrenched off his shirt. "Hold still," he said, but Osorio jumped around, waving his hand, unable to dislodge the scorching gem. He hated to do it, but Max grabbed the detective by the shoulders and wheeled him around until he fell.

They toppled into the water, but Max controlled his own fall. *Martial arts for the win,* he thought. In a swift motion, he locked his arm around Osorio's elbow. It wouldn't take Osorio long to pull loose — Max felt too weakened from all that had happened — so he had to work fast. With his free hand inside the shirt, Max reached down and grabbed the emerald.

"Sorry about this," he said, and ripped the gem away.

Osorio's howls sent the nighttime wildlife bolting for safety. Max jumped to his feet, wrapping his shirt around the emerald several times, and hurried out of the water. He wanted a safe place to set the shirt down, and he needed some distance from Osorio before the man starting swinging punches.

However, instead of anger — once the screams subsided — Osorio lay back in the water, letting the cold numb his hand. "Thank you," he whispered.

Scanning the area, Max saw Punk Girl sitting with her shoulder against a tree trunk. Sandra stood behind, testing the handcuffs — probably for the third time. Max knew that look on her face. She wanted to hurt Punk Girl, have a little vengeance of her own, but she would have to be satisfied with seeing Punk Girl arrested. She checked the handcuffs a fourth time.

Not far away, Brenda sat on the ground, her eyes lost and her face slack. Max wondered if being possessed multiple times had done any mental damage to her. At the least, he thought she might suffer PTSD in the coming months. But for the moment, other than shaken and babying a broken wrist, she looked okay enough.

Drummond hovered nearby. He had pulled his hat low, but Max suspected the ghost performed the same detailed scan of people. And just as Drummond's head perked up, Max's did, too.

"Mr. Carroll," Drummond said as Max thought the name.

They both looked around the area again. Mr. Carroll was gone.

Sandra said, "Let him go."

"Doll, I don't think we should do that."

"We're not done here," she said.

"We're not?"

She gestured to the bundled shirt on the ground. The one pulsing purple heat. "We've got to send Samson Price back where he belongs."

# Chapter 31

BEFORE SHE SAID ANOTHER WORD, Sandra reached down and ripped the ward necklace off Punk Girl. She threw it into the woods. Then, gesturing to the non-warded Punk Girl, she said, "Drummond, would you do the honors?"

Moving in fast, he said, "Even though I'm in a lot of pain, it'll be my pleasure."

He reached out and swiped his hand through Punk Girl's head. The woman stiffened before collapsing. With any luck, she would remain unconscious for several hours.

Sandra gently tapped Brenda's shoulder. "Do you think you're up to giving me a hand?"

"With what?" Brenda still acted cloudy.

"I need help to prepare a complicated spell."

Bounding to her feet, barely wincing at her wounds, Brenda said, "Absolutely." The surprise on everyone's faces must have been clear enough. She shrugged. "In the last week, I've been haunted, possessed, tied up, held at gunpoint, and seen whatever the heck all this Brotherhood stuff was about. Getting the chance to cast a spell with an authentic witch who doesn't want to harm me — I won't turn that away."

Max held back a laugh. Most people had one of two strong reactions to the existence of the paranormal. Either they went to whatever lengths necessary to deny their experience or they embraced it with a surge of zealotry usually reserved for the newly faithful.

"First thing we need to do is clear an area for the spell," Sandra said.

Brenda hopped to work, gathering brush and piling it aside. Her good hand trembled, but she refused to slow down. Sandra walked over to Max. She hugged him with a gentle touch, but he pulled her in tight. Even as he grimaced at the burn in his wrist and the soreness along his back, legs, hips, and arms, he refused to let go. When she finally pulled back and kissed him, he learned his mouth was also bruised.

"How can I help?" he asked.

She kissed him again. "The spellbooks I got at Haven House are in the car. I need the black one with a gold letter *V* embossed on the cover."

"You got it."

Drummond floated closer. "I'll go, too. Last thing we need is for you to trip and twist an ankle."

"How are you going to prevent that?"

"I'm not. But at least I can come back here and let the others know that you needed help. And what an idiot you are."

Heading up the path, Max peeked back and saw Sandra check on Osorio. He continued to nurse his hand in the cold stream, but he also looked more alert. She patted him on the back, urging him to stay still, and then she talked to the empty air above the emerald wrapped in Max's shirt. Samson Price. Max couldn't hear her well, but he had no doubt she explained what she would be attempting, the risks involved, and that he would need to be patient.

"It's okay," Drummond said. "Price has gone through a hellish lot to get this far. He won't screw it up."

As they hiked back up the path and used the concrete slab steppingstones across the water, Max said, "I don't even know why I bother. I'm soaked."

Drummond floated at his side. "We're creatures of habit."

Heading up the incline toward the area Max thought of as basecamp, he heard an odd tinge to Drummond's voice. "What's bothering you?" Max asked.

The ghost gestured back towards the mess they left behind. "That wasn't enough for you?"

"I know you. What's wrong?"

"Nothing," he said, rubbing his hand.

"The wards? It's not your fault they came protected."

"Didn't say it was. I don't blame myself for the magic they brought. But that's the first time I've ever come across a ward so strong. We've seen the Brotherhood digging into some obscure and powerful spells, but they don't have a good batting average, either. They're good at finding these things, not at pulling them off."

Max stopped in front of the sluicing area as the implications hit him. "The Brotherhood could have made wards, but not ones so strong."

"Exactly. Somebody else made those things. Somebody who knows what they're doing. Possibly better than anybody we've come up against."

"Madame Ti?"

Drummond scratched his jaw. "We've dealt with her before. She may have been holding back on us, but it doesn't seem like she's capable of a ward this strong — one that could handle me pounding into it over and over. I don't know. We'll have to talk to Sandra about it, but in the meantime, we need to be extra careful."

They trudged on into the parking lot. Mr. Carroll's car and Osorio's car were both parked next to Max's. "Osorio really came through," Max said. "You did, too."

"Don't get a big head. Osorio merely trailed Brenda and lucked into finding us. And I came for Sandra, not you."

"Wouldn't have it any other way."

Sandra had left her books on the passenger seat. As Max went around the back of the car, he glimpsed the large *V* on the cover of the top book. Hard to miss.

After opening the passenger side door, he leaned in but heard two sounds that stopped him — fast-moving footsteps on the dirt gravel, and his partner yelling, "Look out."

Max whirled around in time to see Mr. Carroll's face red with blood and rage. The small man loomed tall as he raised his walking cane high in the air and chopped downward as if axing firewood. Never before had Max been so thankful for the martial arts training he had been going through over the last years. Without thinking, his muscles reacted.

His right arm went up and at an angle forming a high block that would make his instructors proud. The cane cracked down against his forearm, and momentum flung it off to the side. The blow hurt and would no doubt leave an ugly bruise, but the block had saved Max's head. The next instant, Max brought up his knee and thrust out his foot, snap-kicking Mr. Carroll in the gut. The man tumbled onto his backside.

A few feet further away, Drummond watched. The tension in his shoulders, the desire to leap in and help his partner, strained against the reality that Mr. Carroll's ward prevented him from help of any kind. Not quite.

As Max stepped closer to Mr. Carroll, tight fists at the ready, Drummond said, "Don't be a fool. This is no time for a fistfight. Get your gun."

The ghost was right. Deep in Max's heart, he wanted to pummel Mr. Carroll. That man and his Brotherhood had threatened to take away so much from Max and Sandra. After spending most of the day trying not to die and most of the night trying to accept a curse that might have been worse than death, Max craved to exact far more than a simple pound of flesh.

But to do so risked giving Mr. Carroll an opportunity. To do so meant acting as villainous as Mr. Carroll himself.

Instead, Max listened to Drummond. He turned back to the car and opened the glovebox. His 9 mm — still unloaded — rested atop the car registration. He trusted the threat of the weapon would be enough.

"He's running," Drummond said.

Max turned back in time to catch sight of Mr. Carroll's dirt-stained back dashing into the woods — well, hobbling fast. Max looked to Drummond. "Why didn't you follow him? Keep an eye on where he went?"

But Drummond didn't watch Mr. Carroll at all. Instead, he stared at the dirt road leading away from the mine. "We have company."

Max didn't see anybody. "Where?"

"Another ghost."

"Friend of yours?"

"Never met the guy. But he's not looking too friendly."

"At least we can guarantee one thing — he's not wearing a ghost ward."

Drummond drifted forward a bit, his chest puffing up. "That's far enough, pal. I've had a long night in which I wanted to punch a lot of people and couldn't do any of it. I wouldn't advise playing games with me right now. You want to leave here in one piece, tell me your name and what you want. Or you can do us both a favor and just leave on your own."

After a moment, Drummond shifted back towards Max. "Says he knows you."

Max rested back against the car. "Let me guess — big guy, bushy beard down to about his chest."

"Yeah. Who is this?"

"Marshall Drummond meet Frank Card." Max grabbed Sandra's spell book and gestured for both ghosts to follow him. "Frank, you might as well join us. It's time to break your curse, too."

# Chapter 32

## MONDAY

3 AM. MAX AND SANDRA settled into bed and shared a bottle of chardonnay. No glasses. Just passing the bottle back and forth, each swigging as much as necessary.

Though the spell had taken nearly two hours to set up properly — Sandra had to start over twice — eventually, she had the lines and symbols exactly where they needed to be. According to the spellbook, the casting witch could only perform the spell alone, and the power source had to operate through her. Max didn't like the sound of any of that, but Sandra overruled him. Not that he had much say to begin with. As Drummond pointed out, "We didn't go through all of this to stop right before the finish line." The result — a shock of energy ripped through Sandra leaving her to pant and sweat in the casting circle while Samson Price and Frank Card moved on as they should have done long ago. Together.

Sandra downed two large gulps before handing the bottle over to Max. She opened her mouth to speak, held it open as thoughts bounced around her head, and then closed up. Max watched her, waiting, but when she said nothing and only stared straight ahead, he did the same. In fact, the only words she had spoken since casting the spell occurred when he helped her to the car. She looked up at him and said, "I need a drink."

Brenda had thanked them over and over again before she left, and Max got the sense that her gratefulness went beyond putting Samson Price to rest. He couldn't blame her. After all, she had spent years trying to understand the paranormal and fighting off the doubters. Even the self-doubt. But now, she knew it was all real. She wasn't crazy or foolish or naïve. That alone had to be worth everything she had endured.

For Osorio, however, the cost for having his suspicions proven true turned out to be a lot higher. Though not burned to the bone, the hand that had clutched the emerald had been cursed. Fortunately, Mr. Carroll's full curse never completed casting. While Osorio did not have a skeletal hand with the touch of death the curse had intended, his touch did cause damage. And pain. When he clasped the trunk of a tree to pull himself up the bank, he hissed at the anguish blazing up his hand. And a charred handprint remained on the bark. Nobody dared let his hand brush against them, but the assumption that the pain would hurt both parties was clear.

Max chugged from the bottle and passed it back to Sandra. He wanted to ask her if she had noticed Drummond during the casting. Because he had. When Sandra used the emerald to power her spell, when she opened a bright light that only the ghosts could see, Max had one ghost he could focus on. As the other ghosts passed into the Beyond, he could see the brightness upon Drummond's face.

And, of course, he saw Drummond's expression.

It was similar to before — longing mixed with mournfulness. As if he were alive and standing before a lover's grave, knowing that he would have to wait out the rest of his lifetime before he could be joined with her once again. But he wasn't alive. There was no lover. There was only a world beyond.

Max also wanted to ask Sandra about Haven House. He had been in the strange library for a short time, but already he overflowed with questions. The place could be a great resource, but how much did she know about the witch librarians? And that weird book — how many other books like it sat in that old building? Perhaps he should try to convince Sandra that Haven House was better left in the past. Perhaps he knew better than to open his mouth about such a thing.

Besides, what he really wanted to ask Sandra had to do with the emerald. Because when the spell finished, the emerald no longer glowed. It cracked and several pieces flaked away. Staring at this used up, shattered piece of energy, Max thought about Samson Price. He couldn't simply jump back into the Beyond without that spell. The way Drummond had looked off into that light — twice now — made it clear that he could not simply move on anymore, either.

It seemed like the obvious question — could Sandra create a spell to help Drummond like she had done for Samson Price and Frank Card? Of course, to do so would require a massive energy source like the emerald, and since that one had been used up, they didn't have access to another. Not yet.

But Max stayed quiet. If the day ever came when Drummond tired of the Porter Agency, when he decided he wanted to move on for good, he would tell them. He knew his best chance for such a thing would be Sandra. Until then — Max reached over for the bottle and took another drink.

One of them should get to sleep. They only had a few hours until dawn arrived, and then the routine of daily reality returned. They would have to pick up the boys from Max's mother's apartment. J would be upset that he had missed out on all the fun. Max would fill him in, stressing the danger and how *not-fun* it had all been, but J would be too enamored by the details to listen.

They would have to wait until they were out of PB's earshot. No reason to cause that boy more stress and doubt about the Porter Agency. Later, Max would drive back to visit with his mother. He needed to work out a schedule with her so that everybody knew when Mrs. Porter required their attention. It wasn't fair to the Sandwich Boys to keep disrupting their daily lives.

Max shook his head, chuckled at himself, and grabbed the bottle. He could practically feel PB's accusing stare. Well, so what if there was more to it all than a simple schedule? PB needed to face reality.

*Maybe I need a little of that, too.*

He drowned that thought with the last of the wine. Sandra put out her hand, and Max laced fingers with her. That felt good.

And right. It always did.

"I'm making noise since I can't knock," Drummond said, floating into the room backwards. "Are you two decent?"

Max nearly spit the chardonnay across the room. "What are you doing here?"

"I always patrol the house. Especially after a case. You can never be too careful."

Sandra sat straighter. "Is there trouble?"

"No. But you do have two visitors standing in the driveway."

A few minutes later, Max and Sandra walked out of their house wearing bathrobes. Brenda and Osorio waited at the end of the driveway.

"We couldn't sleep," Brenda said with a sheepish grin. With one arm in a cast from hand to elbow, she fumbled to light a cigarette. "After you left, I went to the hospital and spent a few hours getting this wrist taken care of. Then I met up with Jorge and we went to Denny's to eat and talk. To decompress."

Osorio said, "First, I dropped Ms. Stokes off at the station on a weapons charge. Not much else I can pin on her without bringing everybody here into the station. Since I'm under suspension, she'll probably walk. I called in Ashley's body, too. Anonymously. I've got no idea how I'm going to tell her family. But at least I could apologize to Brenda for thinking she was a murderer."

"And I needed to apologize for ditching him. Then I needed to thank him for tracking me down. And for protecting me while I was possessed. And for saving all of us." She took a long drag. "I still can't believe I'm saying those things knowing it all really happened."

Max glanced down at Osorio's right hand. The man wore a black leather glove now — probably would wear it the rest of his life. Max guessed even a glove caused some level of pain. "You guys came to our driveway to tell us that?"

"Not exactly."

Taking a firm step forward and lifting his head, Osorio said, "After everything, well, I can't walk away from this. Neither can she. We talked about starting our own version of the Porter

Agency, but then Brenda had a better idea."

"I figured why reinvent the wheel? We should talk to you first," she said. "We thought, if you're okay with it, that maybe we can work for you. We could be great assets."

"I'm sorry," Max said, "but we don't have any money to hire anybody."

"Not asking to get paid," Osorio said. "I'm not quitting my job for this. In fact, it's my job that's going to help you. The police come across strange things all the time. Most of it gets filed away or dismissed, but I can bring those cases to you. And when you're working your own cases, I can provide information that wouldn't be available to regular civilians."

Drummond had been floating off to the side but moved in closer now. "Listen to him. I know firsthand that it's a good idea to have a cop on your side."

Sandra said, "If you're offering to help us, we're not going to turn that down. Good help is always appreciated. But like my husband said, we can't pay you. We can barely pay ourselves."

Brenda said, "I won't need to be paid, either. I've got my own job. And I'll do anything you guys need. I'm only looking to be a part of it. I want to help others who might end up going through what I went through." Her face wrinkled as she rolled her lips in and out. "And I suppose I was hoping that maybe you might teach me."

"Teach you?"

"About magic. About how you cast spells."

Sandra laughed. She covered her mouth and shook her head. "I'm sorry. I'm not laughing at you. It's the idea that I could teach you anything. I barely know what I'm doing."

"That's not true anymore, doll," Drummond said. "You're a step or two above being an amateur. You've got the basics down pretty strong from what I can tell."

Max said, "Judging from what the other witches have said, I'm thinking you're further along than that."

Clasping her hands as if in prayer, Brenda said, "Please. I've seen magic for real now, and I can't pretend I haven't. I'm going to quit the Peepers. They're nice people, but this is different. This is the real thing, and they wouldn't believe anything I said. They'd figure I'm making it up to get attention or something. But now, well, I mean — magic. I need to learn how to use it. I'm going to learn how to use it. But if you help me, I feel I'll be safer about it. I've seen that you're a good person. That's the kind of teacher I want. One who will teach me how to use magic in a good way."

Max pointed to his wife. "She's got you there. You've been saying that you want to be a good witch and hopefully make good witches. Now's your chance."

Drummond clapped his hands together once. "That's that then. Looks like the Porter Agency is growing a bit bigger."

"I guess all I can say is welcome to the team," Sandra said.

Brenda hugged Sandra, and Osorio gave Max an awkward left-handed handshake.

Turning back, Max strolled up to the house. "No more of this hanging out in our driveway. The Porter Agency's offices are the kitchen for now, so feel free to join us. No smoking, though. Sorry about that." He paused and looked back. "Very important question for new team members, though, one that will define your role with us."

"What do you want to know?" Brenda said.

"I'll tell you anything," Osorio said.

Max narrowed his eyes. "How do you feel about Lexington barbecue?"

# Afterword

Thank you all for joining me, Max, Sandra, Drummond, and all the rest on another wild ride. If you liked the story, please leave a review wherever you purchased this book. It makes a difference. But you're not reading this to hear my pleas, you want some details of truth, so here we go:

To start with, here's the big one — Hiddenite is a real town, the emerald mine is real, and so is the house/museum dedicated to Diamond Jim Lucas. I first learned of the place many years back when I was a parent chaperone for my son's school trip to go sluicing at the emerald mine. My wife did the same job years later during a second school trip. And finally, while struggling to discover what I would be writing this latest Max Porter book about, my wife suggested we go sluicing for a fun, get-out-of-the-house day. That trip uncovered the Diamond Jim house and its unique story. All the cluttered rooms, the doll collection, art exhibits, and photographs are described as I saw them. The only embellishments were the addition of Samson Price and Frank Card to the photographs.

During that visit, we also found The Yellow Deli because we were hungry and there really are only a couple places to eat in that small town. It was a delicious and unique sandwich place that did not seem to fit, but I'm glad somebody thought it did.

Having said all that — please do not go to Hiddenite in search of a magic emerald. I made that part up, and I doubt the museum folks would appreciate people destroying their walls.

Ashley Cortez's apartment building is actually an empty lot, and Brenda Byrd's is a private home. However, the areas they lived in are fairly accurate. The warehouse is real, too, and while the half-painted wall did exist at the time of my writing this, it is very possible that somebody finally finished it.

Lastly, regarding Haven House, the woods between the local airport and a clump of homes does exist. To the best of my knowledge, there is no secret witch library (I know, I know — don't call it a library) hidden amongst those trees. I did change some of the road layout to better accommodate the story's needs, but these were minor alterations.

# Acknowledgements

While I usually reserve them for the end of this section, I'm starting this time with thanks to my wife and son. This novel owes a lot to them both. First off, the story wouldn't even exist without my wife's suggestion that we spend a day sluicing at Hiddenite. Then, after I wrote the book, I had both my wife and son read the first readable draft. This happens with every book I write and usually results in me fixing numerous minor errors and continuity gaffs. However, this time, they uncovered a major issue that was ruining the second half of the book and required an extensive rewrite. Without their helpful eyes and keen minds, I'm not sure if this book would have happened. I might have had to scrap the whole thing and start over. So, thank you both. Max and the gang are indebted to you. And to my son, since I know you don't often read the published version of these books, I'm offering you $50 if you mention that you read this.

Thanks also goes to Renata Lechner for her beautiful cover work and Darin Kennedy for his continued friendship. Also, a big thank you to the fine people running the Hiddenite Museum as well as those wonderful folks at the Hiddenite Emerald Mine. All the photos they let me take made writing this book infinitely easier. My old brain doesn't remember all the details as well anymore!

And finally, of course, I thank all of you readers. It is a great privilege to create these books for you. Knowing you are out there, waiting for the next one, always brings me motivation when I need it most.

Thank you.

# About the Author

Stuart Jaffe is the madman behind The Max Porter Paranormal Mysteries, the Nathan K thrillers, The Ridnight Mysteries, the Parallel Society novels, The Malja Chronicles, The Bluesman, Founders, Real Magic, and much more. He trained in martial arts for over a decade until a knee injury ended that practice. Now, he plays lead guitar in a local blues band, The Bootleggers, and enjoys life on a small farm in rural North Carolina. For those who have kept count in the past, I'm no longer listing the animals. As we've gotten older, we don't keep the zoo we once did, and it seems silly to list a more normal grouping of pets. So, yeah, we got dogs and cats and chickens (and a couple other things). Still, the chickens will not be permitted in the house.

www.ingramcontent.com/pod-product-compliance
Lightning Source LLC
Chambersburg PA
CBHW030520310726
48979CB00010B/1740/J
* 9 7 8 1 9 6 3 5 1 7 0 8 8 *